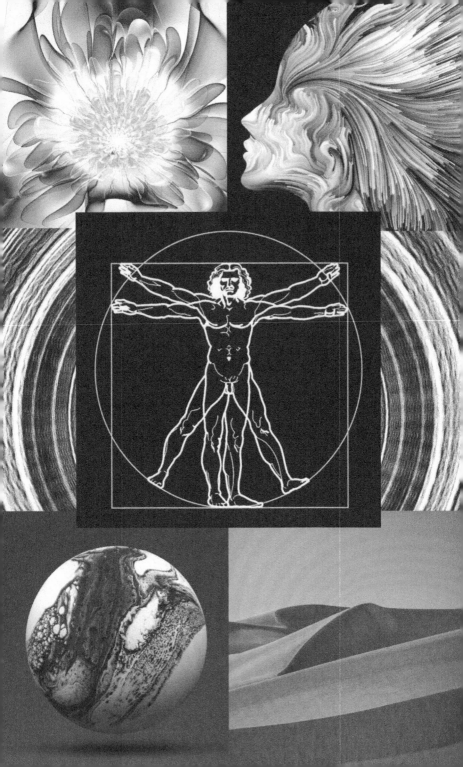

ANTHROS GALACTICA

Episode 1

Rise of the Omicron

By

Erik P. Antoni

A Science Fiction Story

Author
Erik P. Antoni

Editor
Monica Lamb

Cover Designer
Melissa Williams Design

Noetic Press*
Text Copyright © 2020 Erik P. Antoni
ISBN: 978-1-7339063-8-8

Please visit the author's webpage at:
www.songoftheimmortalbeloved.com

<u>Other Books Written by Erik P. Antoni</u>

- The Alchepedia
- Concerto of the Rising Sun
- Song of the Immortal Beloved
    o Mount Sophia
    o Mount Kabbalah
    o Mount Magia

CONTENTS

INTRODUCTION

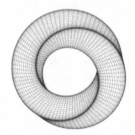

THE ADVENT OF HUMANITY

L ong ago, in the deep eternal past, when the Milky Way Galaxy
was new and sentient intelligent life was just coming of age,
the galaxy was divided and at war. Sentient intelligent life had
found a common human form arising from what nature had determined
to be the perfect balance between pure animal dexterity and a
self-actualizing living awareness.

Several young, but very advanced, spacefaring human civilizations
were in a great struggle with each other fighting for control in
determining the fate and destiny of all life throughout the galaxy. The
most powerful and influential human civilization was the *Orion Empire*.
It ruled hundreds of civilized star systems in the early days of the
Milky Way Galaxy, including the star systems of Orion, Aldebaran,
and the Pleiades. Sirius and its nearby star systems were ruled by a
powerful enigmatic humanoid race called the *Dominion*. The Orion
military was conquering many systems in an attempt to establish order,
peace, and civility throughout the galaxy.

The Orion Empire was ruled by the Bellatrix dynastic royal
bloodline. In power was *King Sah Bellatrix* and his two sons:
Lord Raiden Bellatrix, and *Lord Giao Setairius*. Lord Giao was the
firstborn of King Sah but he was born out of wedlock to King Sah's
most admired consort, *Dianna Setairius*, not to the Royal Queen.

Lord Giao was given the last name of his mother to protect the
integrity of the royal bloodline. Lord Giao, however, was raised
alongside his half-brother, Lord Raiden.

❖ INTRODUCTION ❖

Lord Raiden Bellatrix was the second child born of King Sah but the firstborn in wedlock to *Queen Adoriti Bellatrix*. He was therefore the first in line to succeed his father, King Sah. Raiden was in his prime. Compared to a modern human on Earth, he was a man in his early 40s. He had gained a mastery over both his mind and body. In Earth years, he was actually much older than a man in his early 40s. In the early Milky Way, human beings lived for thousands of years.

Both Lord Raiden and Lord Giao were raised in the royal court by a team of specialists in a variety of fields of study from science, mathematics, history, languages, martial arts, psychology, meditation, biology, military strategy, tracking and survival, political science, engineering, city planning, and governance.

Lord Raiden's personality was polished by his upbringing and nobility. He displayed a profound commitment to principles, ethics, family, and duty. He was known to have a big heart and a strong bond with those he cared for. Raiden's greatest gifts were medical, engineering, and military. He was both a brilliant doctor and a genius military operator. He grew into a fierce military commander.

Having trained his entire life with multiple masters in martial arts, Raiden had a kind of scary supernatural combat ability. He was unbeatable. Not even his brother could defeat him. Lord Raiden's respect by the military forces he commanded was unrivaled and unchallenged. His father, King Sah, had given him total authority over the military, police, science academy, and medical fields.

King Sah focused his other son, Lord Giao, where his talents were greatest. Lord Giao was a natural statesman. He was charismatic and charming. His intellect, however, was dispassionate, calculating, and brilliant. Lord Giao's greatest gift was dealing with people, strategy, and gamesmanship. Neither his father nor his brother could beat him in the games of Chess or Go. He had a profound understanding of psychology, religion, politics, law, and economics. His father appointed Lord Giao to be the Chief Justice of the Supreme Court.

Lord Giao, however, was secretly conflicted. He was jealous of his brother Raiden's full blood right to succession. He felt he was being robbed of his birthright. After all, he was King Sah's firstborn son.

❖ THE ADVENT OF HUMANITY ❖

Lord Giao struggled to reconcile this through the course of his life. He knew, however, how to govern his emotions. He was not prone to sentimental feelings like his brother Raiden. He was biding his time. His goal was to convince his father to make him heir to the empire.

One lesson the cosmos teaches any new humanity is that if they wish to continue and flourish, they must quickly learn how to survive and adapt among a whole host of cosmic threats. There are many cosmic threats ranging from:

1.) Planetary impacts from Asteroids, Comets, and Meteorites,
2.) Solar Storms, Recurrent Novae, and Super Novae,
3.) Super Volcano Eruptions (Caldera Eruptions),
4.) Gamma-Ray Bursts,
5.) Rogue Planets causing gravitational disruptions,
6.) Black Holes,
7.) Alien Viruses arriving on Meteorites or Comets, and
8.) The possibility of another intelligent lifeform being hostile.

Any humanity living on the surface of a planet can be wiped out very easily. For any human race to survive more than 10,000 years, they must learn to mitigate these threats, or another human race must step-in and mitigate for them until they can mitigate on their own. Obvious mitigation measures include:

1.) Build all cities and habitats below the surface of a host planet,
2.) Spread-out among multiple star systems as fast and as far apart as possible,
3.) Reproduce as much as possible,
4.) Build as many starships as possible,
5.) Keep finding new worlds,
6.) Augment and improve the human genome,
7.) Development of new technologies to mitigate these threats, and
8.) Development of self-sustaining habitats. If a large portion of a society is destroyed, the rest of that society needs to continue. The less interdependent a society is, the more resilient it is.

❖ INTRODUCTION ❖

The Orion Empire flourished and became the most powerful human civilization in the galaxy because it was the greatest at adapting, improvising, organizing, preparing, and executing. Out of all the humanities in the galaxy, the Orion Empire did the most to rise up and mitigate against all natural threats and adversaries.

One advantage the Orion Empire had over its foes was that they had a different concept of morality. They did not look at the world through a lens of right and wrong. They looked at the world through a lens of authentic versus false, truth versus fiction, win versus lose, survive versus die. Right or wrong, this made them much faster and more efficient decision-makers which ultimately gave them the evolutionary advantage. For example, they had no moral dilemma in genetically altering their physical bodies to quickly adapt to a foreign ecology on a new world. The Orion were the ultimate trans-humanists. They did have an issue with genetically altering the human mind which, in most cases, they saw caused psychopathy to arise.

Something the Orion Empire learned to do extremely well was to build huge underground cities deep beneath the surface of a planet. They could survive almost any cosmic assault short of reducing an entire planet to dust.

The epic story ahead, told across the Anthros Galactica series, reveals that there is a great secret to the origin and purpose of sentient intelligent life. Sentient intelligent life is not unique to just the planet we call Earth but is spread throughout the cosmos with one universal prime directive. What this prime directive is, the story of its discovery, and the cosmic saga which came to unfold between worlds in the attempt to fulfill it, or deny it, becomes the greatest story ever told.

In this first episode of Anthros Galactica, Rise of the Omicron, the Orion Empire is about to come face-to-face with its most dangerous and most powerful adversary it had ever faced. The cosmic soap opera which came to unfold between the Orion Empire and this new adversary would ultimately change the course of human history throughout the galaxy. It triggered a whole new course of human evolution for all civilizations throughout the Milky Way, ultimately leading to the human civilization we all know today here on Earth.

REFERENCE GUIDE

HUMANITIES OF ANTHROS GALACTICA

*A*nthros Galactica includes many extraterrestrial civilizations from a myriad of star systems. Although they all had different physical bodies, cultures, and languages, there is one common trait which qualified them all as being *Human*. This one trait is that they all possessed a *Human Soul*. They also shared one other common feature. They all shared the same five-pointed, bi-pedal, humanoid form.

Most human beings of the early Milky Way Galaxy were much larger than humans on Earth today. The average height for an early galactic human was seven feet. They also had much longer lifespans. Some had unlimited lifespans because they continuously regenerated.

The early human beings of the Milky Way Galaxy had three sexes. The sexes were male, female, and androgynous. The three states of sexuality reflected the three magnetic forces in the universe, including positive (Yang), negative (Yin), and neutral (Yuan).

The androgynous sexual state was a primordial trait carried over from the primordial universe. In the early galaxy, if someone was born androgynous, they were revered as some form of primordial demi-god.

The primordial universe is a higher-frequency mother universe to the physical universe. The primordial universe overlaps and gave birth to the physical universe. It still exists all-around us to this very day, unseen by the five physical senses of the human being.

The extra-terrestrial humanities listed on the next three pages are the early galactic humanities involved in episode one of Anthros Galactica. All their appearances are described here in one place as a reference guide for the readers. More civilizations join in later AG episodes.

A. Constellation of Orion. Bellatrix Star System. Planet Erawan.

Their physical attributes include:
- Pale white skin with a faint bluish pigment.
- Large protruding cheek and jawbones.
- Large hazel eyes. Dark hair; could be straight or curly.
- Eyebrows are slightly pointed upward on the ends.
- Large straight nose.
- The average height for an Orion is 7 feet tall.
- Descendants of the Anthro-Orionis Primordial Descender race who adopted the Bellatrix star system and seeded it with life.

B. Constellation of Scorpius. M4 Globular Cluster.
Kronos Star System. Planet Serapas.

Their physical attributes include:
- Caucasian skin color with deep emerald-green eyes.
- Muscular body structure with long bony hands.
- Elongated skulls with dark hair. Slightly indented temples.
- Deep voice tones.
- The humans in Scorpius are unusually tall at 8 to 9 feet.

C. Constellation of Draco. Gamma Draconis Star System.
Planet Emcor.

Their physical attributes include:
- The Draco have remnants of reptilian DNA. Their skin is a scaly pale green. They have natural dark patterns on their skin typically along their spines and sides of the face.
- Pointy ears. Thin lips with a large chin.
- Bright golden eyes. Dark hair. Voices have a metallic chime.
- The average height for a Draco is 7 feet tall.

D. Constellation of Lyra. Vega Star System. Planet Katari.

Their physical attributes include:
- Smooth rounded facial features with small indented-ears.
- Violet colored eyes. No hair on the head or body.
- Amphibious. Pale mint green colored skin with a glow.
- Androgynous sexuality. Voices have a neutral gender tone.

E. Constellation of Taurus. Pleiades Star Cluster. Alcyone Star System. Planet Mu.

Their physical attributes include:

- The Moen (humans from Mu) have a very pale, almost translucent, hairless skin, with a luminescent glow.
- High cheekbones.
- Dark slanted almond-shaped eyes.
- Dark thick straight hair on the head.
- The average height for a Moen is 7 feet tall. The women are shorter and have a very feminine form.

The advanced human civilizations of the Pleiades adopted the star cluster as their home star group and terraformed its planets. Depending on which planet, around which star in the Pleiades, the Pleiadeans have some variations in form. Some even have blonde hair. The Pleiadeans from Planet Mu around Alcyone are the most important to Earth, as their DNA is the ancestral DNA behind all the Indian and Pacific Islander races on the planet. In time, the skin tones changed in response to the Earth's ecology. The Pleiadeans founded the ancient civilization of Lemuria on Earth on the continent of Mu in the Pacific Ocean in cooperation with other cosmic ancestors. This was allowed by the Dogu of Sirius to whom the Earth originally belonged. Different major land masses of the Earth rose and sunk over the course of ancient history.

F. Constellation of Taurus. Aldebaran Star System (Alpha Tauri). Planet Liraset.

Their physical attributes include:

- The Aldebaran have light caucasian skin.
- Extraordinarily strong physical form.
- Deep royal blue eyes.
- Bright orange or auburn hair.
- Deep guttural voices.
- Very tall humans at 8 to 9 feet in height.
- The Druid have a blood lineage to the humans of Aldebaran.
- It's important to mention that the Dogu of the Dominion also had a significant influence on the Druid civilization.

G. Sirius Star System. Planet Nome. Dominion Civilization. Primordial Descender Race. The Dogu, Nomoli, or Nommo.

The Dogu of the Dominion are one of the last Primordial Descender Races in the Milky Way Galaxy. They continuously regenerate and have unlimited lifespans; however, they are mortal and eventually die due to reasons other than aging. Depending on the generation, the Dogu have different forms, all of which are androgynous. Earlier generations are more crocodile-like. The most ancient Dogu form is revealed in a future episode. The most common Dogu form is an amphibious human as pictured above. They have a very light aqua-colored skin with protruding dark fisheyes. They can breathe on land and underneath water. The latest generation of Dogu look Asian, however, they maintain many legacy Dogu traits like being able to breathe under water. The Earth originally belonged to the Dogu. All the Asian races on Earth in 2020 are direct descendants from the Dogu of Sirius with Orion and Pleiadean cultural influences.

H. Andromedans from the Andromeda Galaxy

There's a group of beings from the Andromeda Galaxy who are the ancestral human race behind all people of Afro-descent on Earth. The Andromedans were one of the most spiritually-evolved humans in the early universe. They came to help the evolution of humanity in the early Milky Way Galaxy. The Andromedans are one of very few human races ever known to have completed what is called the *Hyperborean Mystery* which involves an integration of the physical and the primordial dimensions of the human being. They are known to be very reserved in their spiritual teachings. They believe each human civilization needs to realize the great mysteries on their own. The Andromedans have always been close allies of the Dominion. They worked closely seeding life throughout the Milky Way Galaxy. The Andromedans, the Dominion, and the Pleiadeans were the key progenitors and architects behind the rise of humanity on Earth. All three have been here all along.

CHAPTER ONE

CHARIOTS OF FIRE

T he Orion fleet is advancing quickly toward the large orange star *Gamma Draconis*. The ships are cruising in a highly synchronized geometric configuration, weaving in and out, bobbing up and down, tightly wrapping the outer gas giants, as they approach the inner solar system of terrestrial worlds.

The ships are surfing the magnetic fields of each passing gas giant, utilizing each planet's gravity to sling shot them forward to the next world. Planet surfing magnetic fields makes the ships much harder to track and engage. The ships know how to mask their signatures within a planet's magnetic field and fly undetected.

The Orion fleet functions under the direction of a collective hive-mind. The ships work together to confuse their enemies much like zebras running together in a herd. The central intelligence guiding the fleet is a combination of a meta-sentient artificial intelligence (AI) working in deep cerebral sync with the commander of the fleet. The technology combines the organic and inorganic to create a system which is greater than the sum of its parts. Ultimately, the human mind is still in charge, but its abilities are greatly enhanced.

The Orion Military has a vast array of warships organized into several classes. The Command Ship launching the assault is staying back at the edge of the solar system while its smaller fleet of attack vessels make an incursion into the Gamma Draconis system.

The attack fleet consists of 1,000 ships divided into 10 squadrons of 100 ships per squadron. The ships in each squadron are exactly the same. These ships are highly unusual. They are thin, monolithic, and diamond-shaped with a black matte finish. They have no windows, no wings, no appendages, no inlets, and no visible engines. They are literally flying black diamond-shaped monoliths.

The ships fly in formation like bees. They twist and turn in a highly synchronized manner. From afar, they look like an array of wind chimes moving and dancing in undulating waves as they make their march forward. The ships amplify and direct gravity waves to propel their craft. There is no internal combustion. With this type of propulsion, a craft moves inside its own gravity bubble. While inside a gravity bubble, the occupants are inside a different realm of existence than the realm in which they are traveling. This cancels inertia. It also allows a craft to transcend time and space and move faster than light.

The Orion military is famous for intimidating its enemies at the beginning of a battle by putting on an acrobatic show with their ships which both mesmerize and terrify the enemy. They do this to warn the adversary. Surrender now or you will surely be defeated. The strategy has worked many times. The Orion military would rather minimize any loss of life. Their goal is not to kill or destroy the enemy, but to integrate their civilizations into the Orion Empire. They have an ethos and a code of conduct. They have a reverence and respect for the humanities they choose to engage and assimilate. Humanities in which they have no interest, they simply pass-by, unless they take an interest in their planets.

The Draco Alliance has insider intelligence of the incoming Orion invasion. Commander *Ian Loria,* of the Draco Alliance, positioned the Alliance fleet on the dark side of the largest moon orbiting the Planet *Miralax,* the furthest terrestrial world from Gamma Draconis. As the Orion attack ships approach the inner solar system, Miralax emerges as a radiant aqua-blue sphere against the backdrop of the massive orange star of Gamma Draconis. Two of Miralax's Draconis lit moons are beginning to appear out of the darkness of space.

The Orion military knows the location of the Draco fleet. Two Orion attack squadrons converge over Miralax's largest moon and immediately reorganize into a perfectly formed arc spanning the moon. Then from one end of the arc to the other, each ship performs a backward summersault, one after one. It creates a moving spiral within the arc of ships. The ships are dancing while putting on an amazing light show. While the acrobatics are ongoing, two more Orion attack squadrons are stealthily approaching the Draco fleet from its rear flank, in the dead of blackness, on the dark side of the Miralax moon.

Commander Loria anticipated the acrobatic show. The Orion fleet was maneuvering exactly as he expected. He and his captains studied several past Orion incursions into different star systems of other civilizations the Orion Empire had assimilated. They anticipated some of the same tactics would be used against them.

Commander Loria purposely placed the Draco fleet deep inside the system to draw the Orion attack ships inward and away from the Orion Command Ship at the edge of the system which was a far distance from their location. The Draco military knew it was a standard operation for the Orion Command Ship to remain back outside the system while the Orion attack ships made their invasion.

The moment the Orion ships begin their acrobatic routine above the Miralax moon, Commander Loria orders his own attack: "*Captain Eido*, launch the fifth fleet now and begin your attack."

A large hangar-bay door opens up on the surface of a small rocky planetoid object orbiting the edge of the solar system beyond the gas giants. It is not too far from the Orion Command Ship. A hornet's nest of Draco attack ships rises-up out of the planetoid and immediately begins attacking the Orion Command Ship.

The Draco were not sure from which direction the Orion Command Ship would approach, so they placed the attack ships inside several planetoid objects along the perimeter of the Gamma Draconis system. Draco's fifth fleet happened to be closest to the Orion Command Ship.

The Orion attack ships deep inside the Draco system at the Miralax moon learn of the attack on the Orion Command Ship. The Orion attack ships approaching from the backside - and the attack ships performing the acrobatics show – suddenly begin striking the Draco fleet while half of the Orion invasion force splits off and races back toward the Orion Command Ship at the edge of the solar system.

❖ CHAPTER ONE ❖

While hundreds of Orion attack ships are racing back toward the edge of the solar system to rescue the Orion Command Ship, the Draco attack ships are wasting no time attacking the Command Ship before the Orion attack fleet arrives. The Orion Command Ship is fiercely defending itself with a barrage of weapons. It is an amazing conflagration of lasers, explosions, and ships on fire.

Lord Raiden is on the bridge of a different Command Ship high above the equatorial plane of the planetary system seated in the captain's chair wearing a headset connecting him to the Orion hive-mind network. He looks calm, well-composed, and deep in thought. He looks more like a man at a chessboard than a man in a firefight. Lord Raiden speaks and says, "Launch the Planet Driller now."

The Orion Command Ship the Draco are attacking is a decoy. It was from this decoy that all the Orion attack ships were launched, but it's not the actual Command Ship leading the invasion.

Lord Raiden knows where the Draco High Council is located. They're hiding deep inside the *Titus Moon*, the eighth moon of the second-largest gas giant in the system. After Raiden makes the launch order, his Command Ship, *the Daedalus*, separates in two parts. The bottom half detaching from the Daedalus is the Planet Driller. It bores a planet from orbit. Planet Drillers are used to build under-ground cities. They vaporize rock at a rate of one mile per minute.

While all the other ships are in fierce firefights at locations far apart in the system, the Planet Driller drops down quietly from the Daedalus. It looks like a giant Mantis insect descending toward the Titus moon. Leading the Planet Driller ship is another squadron of Orion fighters escorting the Planet Driller. The Planet Driller sets up a mile above the Titus moon, right above the location of the Draco High Council and begins firing its powerful laser drill into the moon.

Lord Raiden opens up a commlink and begins speaking to the Draco High Council:

"Draco High Council members, this is Lord Raiden Bellatrix of the Orion Empire. A giant Planet Driller has just begun drilling the Titus moon right above your location. The laser drill should reach you in about three minutes. You have two minutes to call off your attack ships and surrender; otherwise, you will all be destroyed."

The Draco High Council is in total shock. They thought they were actually winning the battle and had outmaneuvered the Orion ships. The Chancellor of the Draco, *Kizor Bayzor,* responds to Lord Raiden,

"Your Majesty, we will surrender if we can make some reasonable terms for our surrender and integration into the Orion Empire."

Raiden responds, "You are in no position to be dictating terms Chancellor; however, I will agree to meet to discuss your terms, but you must immediately call off your ships and surrender. Your people will be handled with dignity and respect." After a few seconds:

"Alright! We agree to surrender. Our ships are being called off," says the Chancellor. The drilling beam immediately ceases.

Lord Raiden says: "Chancellor, an Orion vessel is on its way to escort you to an undisclosed location to discuss terms."

An Orion attack ship descends from the Daedalus to hover within a couple of hundred feet from the surface of the Titus moon where it's in teleportation range. A team of Orion commandos beams down from the attack ship to the Chancellor. They grab the Chancellor and beam him to the Orion attack ship which then swiftly ascends back to the Daedalus, Lord Raiden's Command Ship.

Once onboard, the Daedalus immediately engages its warp drive and vanishes. The Daedalus is headed to *Erawan,* home-world of the Orion Empire in the Bellatrix star system in the constellation of Orion.

The region of space surrounding the Bellatrix star system cannot be approached while moving at warp. There is a massive stellar defense grid encircling the entire Bellatrix star system. It's made up of quadrillions of space probes which together create an impenetrable forcefield around the entire system. A ship can only enter the system through one of 12 celestial stargates. If any ship attempts to pass through the stellar defense grid while moving at warp, it will be deflected and end up thousands of light-years off course.

Lord Raiden's Command Ship, the Daedalus, jumps out of warp only a short distance from the ninth stargate. It's proceeding on impulse power toward the gate.

❖ CHAPTER ONE ❖

Anytime someone arrives at one of the 12 stargates for the first time, they are in total shock and awe. The amount of technology and megastructures surrounding the celestial stargates is breathtaking. Massive space stations surround and form each gate. Glowing etheric ley lines stretching vast distances of space can be seen guiding millions of starships coming and going. The celestial stargate looks like a massive glowing hornet's nest. The megastructures must have taken tens of thousands of years to build and put in place.

When Lord Raiden's command ship materializes outside the stargate, his ship is given an imperial greeting and escort through the celestial gate. Thousands of starships stop and line up on either side of the path of the Daedalus command ship stretching for many miles as they pass through the stargate complex.

The Chancellor is standing alongside Lord Raiden on the bridge while they pass through the stargate. The Chancellor is mesmerized.

He begins speaking but can barely speak:
"How did you all do this? asks Kizor.

"We're builders. We're builders of ships. We're builders of cities, but most of all, we're builders of humanity. We would like the Draco Alliance to be a part of all this, Kizor. Together, we can both be even greater than what we are now," says Raiden.

The Chancellor responds, "Your Highness ..." Raiden interrupts and says, "Please Chancellor, call me Raiden."

"Okay, then please call me Kizor." Kizor continues speaking:

"My people are very proud. We have traditions. We have an identity. We have a history. We have a way of life. We have a culture. We don't want to lose all that," says Kizor.

Raiden responds: "Kizor, I understand. Your people can still keep all their traditions and identities, but ultimately, we all belong to a greater identity. The greater identity transcends all national identities. The greater identity is not Orion or Draco. The greater identity is *human*.

"Until we stop identifying with all our illusionary identities and start acknowledging what we truly are, we cannot grow as a species.

"Would you really deny your children all this? - pointing to the stargate – "just so you can keep singing them the same lullabies?

"You are Draco. But more than Draco, you are a human being. Being human is what is most important. I ask you, what is the purpose of human existence? I have a feeling that the answer to that question is the secret to everything. I'm not sure we really know the answer to that question. We are still trying to figure it all out," declares Raiden.

"I understand your point of view. And, to answer your question, I honestly don't know," says Kizor.

Lord Raiden's Daedalus Command Ship is still gliding through the stargate complex. The Daedalus, although relatively small in size, is immensely powerful. It has a crew of only 100. All ships with a crew capacity greater than 100 are not allowed past the stellar defense grid. All Orion mother ships are stationed outside the stellar grid. This was designed to prevent a Trojan Horse style invasion of the Erawan system. On the *Kardashev Scale*, the Orion Empire would be classified as a Type 2 civilization. The Kardashev Scale is as follows:

Type 1: A civilization possessing the ability to harness all the energy radiating a planet from its host star. Currently, on Earth, present-day 2020, our humanity only generates and consumes about a quarter of the amount of energy hitting the Earth from the Sun, and most of what is generated is not collected from the Sun through solar technology. Earth 2020 is a Type 0 civilization. A Type 1 civilization would have no problem colonizing planets in its own star system. It could also most likely control the weather and earthquakes and be able to implement the large-scale use of nuclear fusion power. Fusion is a different nuclear process than fission which our humanity on Earth today uses in its nuclear reactors. Stars, like the Sun, produce energy through nuclear fusion, not nuclear fission.

Type 2: A civilization capable of harnessing all the energy radiated by its own star. For example, they would be able to build a *Dyson Sphere*. A Dyson Sphere is an artificial megastructure which completely encompasses a star and captures a large percentage of its energy output.

Type 3: A civilization in possession of energy at the scale of its own galaxy. The technology of this type of civilization would possibly be indistinguishable from reality itself. For example, the reality you see around you today could very possibly be all part of a Type 3 civilization matrix of reality controlled by a hidden technology based in a higher dimensional mother universe. Physical organic life itself could be a Type 3 technology. A Type 3 civilization could also theoretically tap into the power of Blackholes, Quasars, and Gamma Ray Bursts.

The Orion Empire measured a civilization in a similar manner as the *Kardashev Scale*, but they called it the *Anthronex Scale*.

Since the time that the three levels of the Kardashev scale were established in 1964 by Soviet astronomer *Nikolai Kardashev*, others have come along to either expand or refine the scales.

Type 4 would be a civilization which can control the energy of an entire universe. Type 5 would be a civilization which could control the collective energy of multiple universes.

Carl Sagan suggested adding another dimension on top of the "pure energy usage" which is the "information available to a civilization." He assigned the letter "A" to represent 10^6 unique bits of information (less than any recorded human culture) and each successive letter to represent an order of magnitude increase, so that a level "Z" civilization would have 10^{31} bits. In this classification, 1973 Earth was a 0.7 "H" civilization, with access to 10^{13} bits of information. Carl Sagan believed that no civilization had yet reached a level "Z."

John Barrow proposed a reverse scale measuring a civilizations' mastery of the very small versus the very large starting with the scale of themselves and then progressing all the way down to the ultimate structure of space-time itself. In this system, there are seven micro-levels.

Robert Zubrin suggested the best way to measure a civilization was by how widespread it was, such as whether if it had spread out across its planet, across its solar system, or across its galaxy. There are also other methods of measurement, such as the level of mastery of systems.

CHAPTER TWO

PLANET ERAWAN

L ord Raiden's Command Ship, the Daedalus, is now beyond the stargate allowing access into the Bellatrix star system. They're cruising past all the outer planets of the system. As the Daedalus approaches the Erawan home-world, a second defense grid arises encompassing the entire Erawan system including its two moons.

They approach another celestial gate. It looks like a giant cosmic doorway into an inner sanctum. It has an ominous feel. At the right and left sides of the stargate are massive space stations shaped like giant columns forming a large doorway. Glowing ley lines light up and take hold of the Daedalus guiding it through the stargate.

There are only three stargates to the inner sanctum through which a ship can pass to enter the actual Erawan domain.

The security to enter the Erawan home-world is impenetrable. Almost no one is allowed to visit. In this case, Chancellor Kizor is Lord Raiden's guest.

As a third measure of defense, no one can teleport down to the planet. There is another defense grid encircling the planet itself blocking all ships and teleportations. You can only take a shuttle to the surface of Erawan, and to enter its atmosphere, you can only enter through the north or south pole of the planet.

No ship can penetrate the defense grid outside the two poles. Once flying in the atmosphere, all ships, including all imperial ships, are forced to land at the landing station below the pole they entered. Any ship veering off course is immediately intercepted. There is no air traffic within the Erawan airspace. It is strictly forbidden. There are no cities or habitats on the surface of the planet. All the cities are located deep beneath the surface. People use underground hyperloops to take them anywhere on the planet within minutes. The surface of Erawan is a pristine paradise for all citizens of Erawan to visit and enjoy. You would never know this was the home planet to one of the most technologically advanced civilizations in the Milky Way Galaxy.

Lord Raiden docks the Daedalus command ship at the Erawan stargate. Raiden and Kizor are walking together through the station on their way to a shuttle which will take them to the surface. Raiden stops to look out some windows to view the beautiful planet Erawan in space.

"Excuse me Kizor, every time I come home, I always stop and take a few minutes to gaze upon my home-world from space. It's still the most beautiful planet I've ever seen," says Raiden.

Erawan looks a lot like Earth except it has soft pink and lavender swirls. It looks like a glowing marble of blue, white, pink, and lavender. The pink and lavender colors come from special minerals abundant on Erawan but not found on Earth, or anywhere else. These minerals have amazing rejuvenating properties.

Raiden and Kizor board the shuttle and immediately depart the station and begin gliding toward the north pole of the planet. Two ships appear on either side of the shuttle guiding it to the landing station.

The shuttle is now free-floating downward toward the station. Suddenly a massive hole opens up at the top of the planet. They descend into a giant cavern. At first, it's total darkness, and then suddenly it's full of city lights with little craft buzzing all around.

Again, Kizor cannot believe what he is seeing.
Raiden says: "You haven't seen the best part yet, Kizor."

"You have to be kidding me," replies Kizor.

They stop their descent and begin flying forward, twisting, and turning, like flying through a great canyon, and then suddenly they enter a great expanse with gleaming sunlight. There is green land below them wrapping and curving upward into a mist.

"Oh my God, you have a whole surface world beneath the planet," says Kizor.

Kizor continues: "How did you get the sunlight to penetrate and radiate the inside of the planet? Is this some kind of projection?"

"It's not a projection, It's real natural sunlight. It's the science of *Fractal Resonance.* To explain it very simply, we bring the area of the planet we wish the sunlight to penetrate into harmonic resonance with the sunlight until the material separating the sunlight from our location becomes translucent allowing the sunlight to pass through. But all the rocky material of the planet is still there. It just allows the sunlight through," explains Raiden.

"You literally have a whole living, breathing, planet beneath the planet with a fully developed civilization," says Kizor.

"Yes, we have over a billion people living deep inside the planet. We have a fully sustainable habitat inside the world. We've been here for over a million years," says Raiden. (1.00 Erawan year = 1.25 Earth year)

The shuttle softly touches down alongside a lake in front of a beautiful villa. Standing outside waiting for Lord Raiden and his guest are his father, King Sah, and his older brother, Lord Giao.

King Sah looks like the Ancient of the Days with long gray curly hair falling past his shoulders and a high forehead.

Raiden is very fit and muscular. He has black hair combed straight back with a slight part on the side. His face looks chiseled with protruding cheekbones and a large chin.

Giao is two inches shorter than his younger brother with a body like a runner. He has black curly hair almost touching his shoulders.

Kizor is medium-sized with short gray hair.
Raiden and Kizor walk out of the ship. King Sah and Lord Giao are visibly pleased to see them both. King Sah says:

"Welcome Chancellor. For a long time, I have been wishing for the day that you would visit us. I am so happy and pleased you are here. We have much to discuss."

King Sah looks over at Raiden giving him a subtle gesture and nod of approval for a job well done. King Sah and the Chancellor walk ahead of Lord Raiden and Lord Giao.

Lord Giao and Lord Raiden are walking and talking quietly about 15 feet behind King Sah and the Chancellor. Lord Giao remarks:

"Very well done my brother. Your misdirection strategy was brilliant, especially having half of the Orion attack ships at the Miralax moon race back to save the decoy command ship.

"It created the perception in the Draco's minds that their strategy was working, totally misdirecting them for what you were about to do next," says Lord Giao.

"Thank you, Giao. A lot of that strategy comes from you. You are a master at creating a false reality to misdirect your opponent.

"I learned from you that it's not enough to just create a false reality. You must help your opponents to confirm their false reality, to help them truly believe in it, and then you have them.

"The ships racing back to save the command ship confirmed their false reality," says Raiden.

King Sah, Lord Giao, Lord Raiden, and the Chancellor talked inside the Villa for many hours. They allowed the Chancellor to contact the High Council of the Draco Alliance to let them know he was okay and that he was being treated very well as an honored guest. He was allowed to inform the High Council that he was on Erawan.

The Chancellor had many mixed feelings. He was deeply impressed by the royal family and all that he had learned and had seen, but at the same time he had to keep reminding himself that the forces of the Orion Empire were now the conquerors of the Draco Alliance.

He was very careful not to show too much interest in what the royal family had to offer.

They all decided to take a break to think about their talks. In the morning they would reconvene for a final discussion. King Sah stands up to introduce Kizor to someone.

"Kizor, you are the most honored guest in our home this evening, please allow me to introduce you to *Farah Nuor*. Farah is the Queen's Chief of Staff and Manager of the Villa. She will make sure your stay is as comfortable as possible. We brought in a Draco chef to prepare anything you may wish to eat. Let's meet again in 12 hours," says King Sah.

Kizor nods to the King in agreement and then looks to Farah to show him the way to his quarters.

Kizor and the royal family had no problem talking. They were all using a universal translator. It's a tiny pin placed behind the ear to interface directly with the brain.

When people are speaking a different language, you hear what they are saying in your own native language, and when you are speaking, they hear you in their own native language.

Kizor and Farah are walking down a corridor to his quarters. While walking, he is startled to see a little person who is literally only several inches tall with little clothes, a really cute face, and spikey hair looking up at him smiling with a warm glow about her.

Kizor remarks and asks Farah:

"Oh my God, a little person. What is that?"

Farah answers:

"Oh, that's a *Cherub*. They are meta-sentient little beings. We let them come and go as they please. They are indigenous to Erawan. Did you get a look at our planet from space?" asks Farah.

"Yes," says Kizor.

"Did you see the pink and lavender swirls?" asks Farah.

"Yes, I saw them, they looked so beautiful," says Kizor.

"Those minerals have only been found on Erawan. They were produced by the Bellatrix star and somehow when Erawan emerged as a planet, these incredibly rare minerals were carried with it. They're part of the planetary consciousness. The Cherubs are little meta-sentient lifeforms which arose and evolved in connection with these minerals. These minerals and the Cherubs are very sacred to us. Please treat them with the utmost respect. The fact that you saw one, and she smiled at you, is a great sign. I will let the King know," says Farah.

"What are the names of these minerals? And what do you do with them? Do you consume them?" asks Kizor. Farah replies:

"The soft pink mineral is called 'Era' and the lavender mineral is called 'Wan.' Together, they form the name of the planet, 'Erawan.'

"We don't collect, use, consume, or trade them. It's strictly forbidden. You can touch them, walk upon them, and bathe with them, but they are always left in their natural habitat. I should not say anymore. The subject is very sacred to us," says Farah.

"Thank you for sharing this with me, Farah," says Kizor.

"Wait, why was the little Cherub wearing clothes?" asks Kizor.

Farah explains:

"The Cherubs like to copy and imitate humans. It's one of their endearing attributes. There are different classes of cherubs. What you just saw is a *Cherubitic Gnome,* but we also have Cherubitic Sylphs, Undines, and Salamanders," says Farah.

Meanwhile, Lord Raiden is happy to be home. He walks up behind his wife, *Princess Chae Bellatrix*, and gives her a big hug from behind.

"My love, I am home. I missed you so much," says Raiden.

Chae is excited that her husband has finally returned home. She turns right around and gives him a big long hug and a kiss.

"Raiden, my dear, you have been away for so long, can you stay for a while? Oren's birthday is only two weeks away, he really needs to spend more time with you. He's always talking about you. You should see how well he's doing with his martial arts training. Sensei says he is doing extremely well and that he takes right after his father," says Princess Chae.

"Excellent, I cannot wait to see. Yes, of course, I will plan to stay for a while," says Raiden.

Later that evening Raiden decides to take a walk and visit the old Sensei, *Sensei Oshi Nakamura,* who is training his son, Oren.

Raiden trained with several masters of the martial arts throughout his life, but Sensei Oshi remained his favorite and was a father figure.

It's in the early evening and night has fallen. Raiden is taking a stroll through his village. It's very peaceful. He hears from far away, the sound of children playing off in a distance. He begins reminiscing.

The same garden paths are still there from his youth. He's walking while lightly touching his hands atop the long grass growing along the path. He remembers doing the same as a young boy. It all feels and smells the same. The garden paths are lit with the same little gas-fired lanterns sitting atop of bamboo posts spaced along the garden paths. Raiden looks up and sees all the stars. The same technology allowing the sunlight through also allows the night sky to come through.

The star, Betelgeuse *[bay-tul-gice],* is prominent in the night sky.

Raiden enters a garden courtyard behind a little wooden house belonging to Sensei Oshi. Oshi is there sitting cross-legged on his back-porch cutting vegetables with a big knife. Raiden quietly walks up to him out of the nighttime darkness. Oshi looks up and sees Raiden. He immediately stands up straight with his arms at his sides with a serious look on his face. He's looking down bowing his head out of respect. You can see he's holding back a smile. He is so happy to see Raiden.

"Sensei, it's okay. At ease. I just come to say hello," says Raiden.

They both smile at each other and stare for a few seconds. Raiden takes the formal position before a sparring match and gives a courtesy bow. Oshi immediately does the same. Raiden begins his sparring attack. Oshi is blocking all of Raiden's attacks but he's really impressed by Raiden's speed. Oshi grabs Raiden's arm and pauses to look at it. It's like steel. Oshi gives a nod of approval about Raiden's arm's strength. Then Raiden grabs him and gives him a big hug.

"It's been too long Oshi. How are you? What are you cutting?" asks Raiden

"Oh, I'm cutting zucchinis for a soup I'm about to make. It will be ready tomorrow if you want to come back for some?" asks Oshi.

"Of course, I will. I always loved your soups," says Raiden.

"Oshi, I just arrived home earlier today. I've been away on a special mission for two years. I haven't gone to see Oren yet. I wanted to stop and see you first and ask how his training is going," says Raiden.

One Orion year is how long it takes Planet Erawan to orbit the Bellatrix star. (1.00 Orion year = 1.25 Earth years)

"I can honestly tell you; he is exceeding my expectations every day. Oren trains extremely hard just like you did at his age. He reminds me so much of you. One of these days he's going to land me on my ass! He's almost there!" says Oshi as he laughs out loud!

"Great! As a father, it makes me so proud to hear that. Hey, I have an idea. Tomorrow morning, can you set up a sparring match between me and Oren? Bring him to the dojo. I will be standing there in a mask. Tell him I'm his new sparring partner. Don't tell him it's me. Let's have a little fun," says Raiden.

"Okay," says Oshi, while chuckling.

❖ CHAPTER TWO ❖

It's early the next morning. King Sah, Lord Raiden, and Lord Giao have reconvened for their final talks with the Chancellor.

"Good morning Chancellor, did you rest well?" asks King Sah.

"Yes, for some reason I had the most restful sleep I've had in a long time. I'm not sure why. I'm here, essentially as your prisoner and you have just overthrown our government," says Kizor.

For some backstory context, for many years there was a political movement among the Draco people for the Draco Alliance to join the Orion Empire. The Draco and the Orion civilizations have a lot in common and already conducted a lot of trade. Most people in the Draco civilization feel oppressed and like they have no voice. The political climate has become poisonous. The politicians no longer represent the people. Most are corrupt and taking bribes by lobbyists.

Even worse, what was once a free and trusted media, has become split with each side taking sides between warring political parties. No one knows the truth any longer. The Draco Alliance was headed toward an all-out civil war. The Orion Empire stepped in when they did to prevent a human catastrophe and to ensure the continuation of trade.

King Sah didn't like the Chancellor's "overthrow" and "prisoner" comments and responds:

"Kizor, the truth is, the Orion Empire did not just conquer the Draco Civilization. We got involved to prevent a human catastrophe.

"You know, and we know, you were about to start an all-out civil war. The Draco Alliance is creating instability in the galaxy and the potential loss of human life is not acceptable to us. If the Draco Alliance had its house in order, we would not be here today Kizor. You gave us no choice. Almost all civilizations the Orion Empire have integrated over the last 100,000 years were integrated when they were about to fall apart and send the galaxy into a state of great peril.

"Other human civilizations should watch and take note. If they don't respect human life and work to maintain peace and stability, then we will step in, and when we step in, it's to integrate, it's not to play cop or mom and pop. We don't have time for that.

"The Draco chaos has been going on for far too long. For over 2,000 years Kizor! Enough is enough!" says King Sah.

Chancellor Kizor Bayzor responds:

"Dear, King Sah, Lord Raiden, and Lord Giao, with your permission, last night, I and the rest of the High Council of the Draco Alliance discussed the situation and have produced our own proposal which we can live with. Our proposal is:

1.) The Draco Alliance maintains its sovereign independent status. However, we enter into a treaty with the Orion Empire giving the Orion Empire full oversight over all our cosmic trade affairs. Where there is a dispute, the Orion Empire will be the final arbitrator.

2.) There will be no Orion military vessels in Draco space.

3.) We are willing to pay a 2% cosmic trade tax to the Orion Empire for all goods traded between interstellar humanities. The currency used to pay this tax will be Element 115.

4.) The Orion Empire will not involve itself in our internal political affairs.

5.) The Orion Empire will be given the Miralax moon, *Sikes.* It is the largest of the Miralax moons. It will be a celestial embassy and outpost. It will be your sovereign territory.

6.) Once every Orion year, the Orion Empire will be allowed to conduct an audit of all our cosmic trade transactions."

After listening to the Draco High Council proposal, King Sah calls for another recess to confer with his two sons, Raiden and Giao.

The three have a lengthy conversation and then Lord Giao goes to work drafting an official Orion resolution of terms.

After two hours, they all regather in the conference room. This time Lord Giao takes the lead in the discussion.

Lord Giao was quite the statesman. It was in moments like this that he shined the most. The response was drafted mostly by Lord Giao with edits from his father and brother.

Lord Giao reads the terms:

❖ CHAPTER TWO ❖

"Dear Chancellor, and members of the Draco High Council. You have many good ideas. We accept some of your terms, but we have added a few of our own. All terms shall be as follows:

1.) Your sovereignty shall continue but as a subordinate power of the Orion Empire. Your laws must fall in line with the Orion Constitution which we will provide you. You can create and modify all your laws at your own will, so long as they fall within the boundaries of the Orion Constitution.

2.) The Orion Empire will immediately teach the Draco how to feed, clothe, and provide free energy and medicine to all the Draco people. Food and medicine are already being molecularized through our technology and are already en route to all your planets. We will wipe out disease and poverty on all your worlds just like the rest of the Orion Empire.

3.) You must agree to integrate the entire Draco military and all its bases with the Orion military. There shall be no militias.

4.) As you proposed, you will pay a 2% cosmic trade tax to the Orion Empire for all goods traded between stellar humanities. The currency used to pay this tax will be Element 115. The set value will be the value set by the intergalactic trade federation.

5.) Also, as you proposed, the Orion Empire will not involve itself in Draco's internal political affairs. We only add to this, so long as these affairs do not violate the Orion Constitution.

6.) Again, as you proposed, the Orion Empire will be given Sikes, the largest Miralax moon. It will be a federal Orion territory. No Draco ships or personnel will be permitted on Sikes without the explicit consent of the Orion Empire.

7.) As you proposed, once every Orion year, the Orion Empire will conduct an audit of all Draco cosmic trade transactions. The audit will occur every Draco year beginning on the first day of the eighth month on the Draco calendar.

8.) All Draco institutions and religions are allowed to continue peacefully so long as they do not seek to subvert the authority of the Orion Empire.

9.) From this point forward, all licensed media are no longer allowed to choose political sides and purposely stoke civil unrest. Licensed media are only allowed to report corroborated and well-researched facts. The licensed media itself must be held to a higher standard of responsibility than the rest of the civilian population. All 'non-licensed media' have the same free speech as the rest of the public. The Orion Empire will appoint an off-world third party media monitor who has no vested interest in the outcome of any Draco situation.

10.) All human beings have equal rights regardless of race, gender, creed, or sexual orientation. All human beings have the right to self-determination.

11.) All laws made by the government, apply to the government. No one is above the law.

12.) All elected officials shall have term limits.

13.) Elected officials will not earn money while in elected office. All assets, and all bank accounts, will be the same amount the day they leave office as the first day they entered office, and for ten years thereafter. (1.00 Draco year = 0.70 Earth years)

14.) All current elected officials are allowed to stay in office until the end of their current terms and then they must leave. Starting the next term, the monetary rule shall take effect.

15.) All currency must be backed by a scarce and valued resource possessing intrinsic value such as Element 115. Many ships utilize Element 115 for their gravity propulsion systems. It, therefore, has intrinsic value. We will transform your monetary system to match the Orion system. The current Draco currency will be phased out for a new currency.

"Kizor, we will give you and the Draco High Council one Erawan day to review and accept these terms.

"If not, we will reject all these terms, declare martial law, disband your government and your military, and you and the high council members will remain under house arrest for an indefinite period of time," says Lord Giao. Kizor responds:

"Very well. You will have our response within one Erawan day. Would you mind if I stayed in my quarters between now and then to discuss this with the high council members on an encrypted channel as I did last evening? And would you please give me a copy of the Orion Constitution? Most of the council members are already familiar with it due to previous campaigns to seek membership in the Orion Empire. I want to restudy it today," says Kizor. Lord Giao replies:

"Yes, this is acceptable to us. A copy of the Orion Constitution is actually in your quarters already on the bookshelf. There is a pair of reading glasses on the desk in your quarters. If you put them on, the lens will sync with your universal translator and the text will appear to your eyes in your native Draco language," says Lord Giao.

It's now mid-morning and Lord Raiden is excited to see his son Oren. He has not seen him in two years. Relative to humans on Earth, Oren would be about 18 years old. Raiden is very polite and says his farewell to Kizor and then quickly heads off to the dojo. He needs to get there before Oshi and Oren arrive. He sends Oshi a message that he is on his way. Oshi and Oren are walking together on their way to the dojo. Oshi says to Oren: "I have a new sparring partner for you today."

"Oh, come on Oshi, every sparring partner you brought me in the last year I knocked out in 100 seconds. Only you can give me a real workout now," says Oren.

An Orion minute has 100 Orion seconds. An Orion hour has 100 Orion minutes. One Orion day has 30 Orion hours. One Orion year has 400 Orion days. Orion time is all based on Planet Erawan's spin and orbit.

"Yes, this is true, but this time I think this sparring partner will give you a good workout," says Oshi.

"Oshi, I'm going to take out this person of yours inside of 50 seconds just to show you," says Oren

"Okay, just for saying that, if you don't, then afterward I will make you do 20 Kawasakis," says Oshi.

"What? Are you kidding me? I can barely do 10 Kawasakis," says Oren.

"Well, I guess you better beat him inside of 50 seconds then," says Oshi.

Oren and Oshi approach the dojo. It's a separate little wooden building behind the garden courtyard at Oshi's house. They step inside. Standing at the far side of the room on a mat is Raiden dressed in all black wearing a black hood pulled over his face with a see-through mesh facemask. He looks ominous. He's just standing there waiting for Oren. Oren drops his bag and walks onto the mat approaching Raiden. No words are spoken. Oren has no idea it's Raiden. Sensei Oshi walks to the side of them about 15 feet away to observe. Oren lines up five feet in front of Raiden. Oshi makes a hand signal to begin. Oren and Raiden both take bows.

Oren wastes no time and goes right at Raiden with punches to his body and lunging kicks to Raiden's legs. Raiden is moving and blocking all the shots with grace and ease.

In the midst of the punching, kicking, and blocking, Oren tries a basic Judo takedown called "O Soto Gari."

Raiden sees it coming and spins around to the back of Oren, knocks him down, and pulls Oren's head back with his two hands while putting his knee in Oren's back. Oren is now beet-red, laying chest-first on the mat and flopping his hands like a seal. Raiden holds the position for few seconds and then lets Oren go. Oren quickly stands up, turns around and says: "What the F#%K!"

Oren is in shock at how good his sparring partner is. He's never fought anyone this good before. You can see newfound respect in Oren's face.

Oren goes at Raiden one more time, and this time, Raiden puts Oren in orbit. Oren somersaults in the air and lands on his back. Oren stands up again with his hands at his side, amazed, staring at Raiden. He's thinking, who could this be? Wait a second. There is only one man this good. Oren speaks, "Dad, is that you?"

Raiden drops his mask with a big smile.

"It is you!" says Oren.

"Yes, it's me! says Raiden. Raiden gives Oren a big hug and says, "I missed you, Oren! Wow! You are four inches taller and much stronger since I last saw you. Your training has come a long way!"

Raiden and Oren are walking off the mat and Oren says: "Dad, I want a rematch."

"Yes, of course. Every day you and I will train together while I'm home. I have a lot to share," says Raiden. "Excellent," says Oren.

Oshi interrupts and says: "Wait, Oren, you owe me 20 Kawasakis!" Oshi explains to Raiden about their bet. Everyone is laughing!

Raiden says to Oren:

"You see, it's always when you think you can't get better that someone comes along and puts you on your ass. It's a law of the universe. You must always keep training and preparing for the one who can beat you because you never know when you may meet that person. If you keep that mindset, you may never actually meet that person, and that's the goal. If you change that mindset for a minute, I promise you, you will meet that person," says Raiden.

That evening, there is a family reunion at the royal villa. Many guests are there, mostly relatives and close friends. The entire royal family is in attendance including King Sah, Queen Adoriti, Lord Giao and his concubine Desa Maggis, Lord Raiden and Princess Chae, Lord Giao's mother, Countess Dianna Setairius, and Prince Oren and his lady-in-waiting, Aria Solis. Aria Solis is the woman the royal family hopes Oren will marry to continue the Bellatrix bloodline.

The Bellatrix bloodline is in direct descent of a *Primordial Descender Race* no longer in existence in the Milky Way Galaxy. A Primordial Descender Race is a race of humans who have literally crossed over from the primordial universe into the physical universe billions of years ago to bring life into the physical universe.

They're not completely physical. The name of the descender race the Bellatrix bloodline descends from is *Anthro Orionis*. As previously stated, the primordial universe is a higher frequency mother universe to the physical universe. Planet Erawan was the last world on which the

Anthro Orionis was known to exist. The Bellatrix bloodline is the last remaining master bloodline atop a small group of secondary bloodlines with genetic remnants of Anthro Orionis. To carry the Bellatrix name, your mother or father must be a Bellatrix and the other side must come from one of the secondary bloodlines carrying genetic remnants of the Anthro Orionis DNA.

The reason this is important is that the Orion Empire believes the Human Soul follows the blood in a reincarnation cycle. They believe the Human Souls of their ancient Anthro Orionis ancestors will continue to reincarnate through the Bellatrix family bloodline if the bloodline stays pure. They believe King Sah, Lord Raiden, and Prince Oren are all souls who once lived among the ancient Anthro Orionis in past lifetimes. They are the reincarnation of their godlike ancestors.

The families of Aria Solis, Princess Chae, and Queen Adoriti, are all verified secondary bloodlines with Anthro Orionis DNA. Because of this, they're allowed to marry into the Bellatrix family. In the case of Countess Dianna Setairius, her family is not a verified secondary bloodline. This is why Lord Giao cannot carry the Bellatrix name. However, his concubine, Desa Maggis, is verified.

This is the origin behind what became the horrible malignancy of human racism. The tracking was unnecessary because the truth is, all Human Souls are equal. The Human Soul is not even measured. It is the intercessing principle between creation and the divine source from which everything originally emerged. How this becomes known is told in the episodes ahead. How racism originated on Earth follows the same principle, but they weren't tracking back to a primordial descender race. They were tracking back to something different. This is all revealed later as the Anthros Galactica series unfolds.

There were other Primordial Descender Races in the Milky Way Galaxy. Anthro Orionis was not the only descender race. At this point in time, there was one other known human race in the galaxy whose DNA was actually much more intact from its ancestral Primordial Descender Race. In fact, this humanity was still considered an actual Primordial Descender Race. This humanity was known as the *Dominion.* The Dominion people are called the *Dogu,* or the *Nomoli.*

The Dominion headquarter home-world is in the Sirius star system. Their home-world is called *Nome.* The Dominion moved into the Sirius system. Amazingly, they brought their Planet Nome with them. Nome is extremely special. The story of Nome is told later in the Saga.

The party does not look like a formal royal dinner. It looks like a very informal family gathering. There are about 40 people both sitting and standing in the large open living room with an outdoor terrace. There is light classical music playing in the background. There's a lot of laughter and socializing taking place. Servers are walking around with cocktails and hors d'oeuvres. Giao is making his way around the room like a butterfly putting on his famous charm. Giao's mother, Dianna, always seems like she's up to something. You can see her whispering in others' ears as she stares across the room at people. Princess Chae is very cheerful walking around the room with Raiden. Queen Adoriti is sitting next to her husband King Sah as various people approach them. Queen Adoriti has a remarkable beauty for her age. She doesn't like idle small talk and large parties are a bit too much for her. She always keeps her distance from Dianna. Oren and Aria are with other friends their age laughing and telling jokes.

During the party, two serious official-looking women, obviously not friends and family, walk into the room to see Lord Raiden. They're dressed in all-black. Raiden excuses himself as they walk out to the terrace where it's quieter and they can talk privately.

"Raiden, sorry to interrupt your party, but there's more trouble in Scorpius," says one of lady secret service agents.

"What's the problem Kira?" asks Raiden.

"Our sources are telling us that there's been an insurrection in the Scorpius star system and its military and government are collapsing. We believe the *Omicron Order* is behind the insurrection," says Kira.

"My gosh, the Omicron Order. It was said the Omicron Order was vanquished long ago. If I remember correctly, the Omicron Order was a group of genetically engineered metahumans. They had a religion based upon the fashioning of a genetically enhanced superhuman. Any people they deemed inferior, they sought to wipe out. Psychopathy always arose alongside their genetic enhancements of the mind.

"Ironically, in their effort to create a more superior human, they lost their humanity in the process," says Raiden.

"Yes, Sir. That's correct. You know your history well," says Kira

Kira continues:

"Sir, we believe we may have also identified the leader of the Omicron Order. We believe it's *General Cyrus Urlex*," says Kira.

"Kira and Jes, thank you for coming to see me. Please get the intelligence team together and prepare a full debrief on the situation for me, my father, and my brother. Let me know when you are ready," says Raiden.

Raiden rejoins the party stepping back into a conversation with his wife, Chae, and their friends. King Sah and Lord Giao both look over at Raiden. They're looking for a signal that everything is okay. He looks back with one eyebrow raised signaling that everything is *not okay*.

A few minutes later, Giao makes his way over to Raiden. Raiden whispers into Giao's ear. "Problem in Scorpius. The Omicron Order. Intelligence is preparing a full debrief for us," says Raiden.

Giao listens keenly and then quickly moves on with a big smile and a gracious hello to another friend he hasn't seen in a while.

Dianna is keeping an eye on her son. She is a strong advocate for him. She's always secretly pushing Giao to assert more of his own authority. She has the same goal. She wants her son to be made the official heir of the Orion Empire.

Later that evening, Raiden is sleeping. He's having a dream. He's hiking in the desert. The sun is beating down on him. He slips on some rocks. He's hanging from a cliff. While climbing back up, there's a Scorpion lunging at him trying to sting him. He's hanging by one hand struggling. He looks up. His son Oren is reaching down with one hand trying to help him back up. He wakes up in a cold sweat. He looks over to see his wife, Chae, sleeping.

The next morning. King Sah, Lord Raiden, and Lord Giao are assembled. Chancellor Kizor of Gamma Draconis enters their chamber to deliver the High Council decision on the Orion ultimatum. It's exactly one day later. They're all seated in a conference room with a big window overlooking the lake. The sun is gleaming through. It's a beautiful day.

Chancellor Kizor Bayzor speaks:

"Dear, King Sah, Lord Raiden, and Lord Giao,
the Gamma Draconis High Council agrees to all your terms so long as
three additional terms can be added of our own:

1.) Chancellor Kizor will be appointed interim governor of the
Gamma Draconis system of planets. He shall remain Governor
for four Draco years at which time a new election will be held.

2.) The members of the Draco High Council are included as
members of the transition team.

3.) The Orion Empire will teach the Draco the science of Fractal
Resonance so they can bring the light of their star into their
underground cities as you have on Erawan."

King Sah, Lord Giao, and Lord Raiden all look at each other and
nod their heads in agreement.

King Sah stands up and says:

"Dear Governor, Kizor Bayzor, we would be honored to shine the
light of your sun upon all your people. We welcome the Draco people
into the Orion family. On this day, we have become one.

The royal family and Governor Kizor spent another hour together
signing the final terms of the integration agreement which would be
formalized and readied for signature by all members of the Draco High
Council. They also drafted a roadmap of the next steps. Lord Giao
appointed one of his senior ministers to lead the transition team and
report directly back to him.

After the meeting, Kizor was taken back to Gamma Draconis.
He would return to Erawan in two weeks with the other members of the
Draco High Council to meet the royal family and the rest of the
transition team at which time they will conduct their first transition
meeting.

The base of operations for the transition team will be the Miralax
moon, Sikes. All transition meetings after the first meeting will be on
Sikes. As agreed, Sikes is now a lunar embassy and a sovereign federal
territory of the Orion Empire.

CHAPTER THREE

A TALK WITH DR. RISA LEE

R aiden was happy to get another break from his formal duties to spend more time with his son, Oren. Raiden trained and sparred with Oren for two hours in the dojo, but afterward, there was someone special Raiden wanted Oren to meet.

"Oren, I would like you to meet another old instructor of mine, my meditation instructor, *Dr. Risa Lee*. Do you have a couple of hours after our workout today?" asks Raiden.

"Yes, of course. That sounds great," says Oren.
After their workout, Sensei Oshi served them soup and Oshi told some funny stories to Oren about his Dad when he was younger.

Raiden and Oren were now on their way to meet Dr. Risa Lee. Risa is a doctor in *Psychology* and *Cognitive Harmonics*.

Cognitive Harmonics is a mainstream field of study in the Orion Empire. It explores the psychological integration of the human mind based upon the universal law of sympathetic resonance.

"Oren, what you are about to learn today is more important than your martial arts training. In fact, it's the most important discipline you will ever learn in your life. It will make everything you do better, including your martial arts. It will train your mind to transcend and overcome adversity by overcoming yourself. One of the secrets to overcoming any adverse situation is realizing that the biggest obstacle in any situation is you, it's not the people you are dealing with, and it's not the situation itself. It is easier to change the way we interface with the world than it is to change the world," says Raiden.

"Wow, that's deep. I am looking forward to this," says Oren.
Oren and Raiden are walking toward a park. Standing in front of them up ahead is a woman. She is standing very politely waiting.
As they walk up to her, she gives them both a courtesy bow.

She looks at Raiden and says, "Your Majesty, it's so good to see you again. It's been a long time."

She turns to Oren and says, "Prince Oren, it's so nice to finally meet you. You look so much like your father."

Raiden says, "Risa, it's so good to see you again. Thank you for coming on such short notice. And please, Raiden and Oren will do. We're your friends."

"I found a nice quiet place for us to sit together below a big shade tree. We can do our first lesson there," says Risa.

They walk to the park to find some chairs below a big tree. There was some initial catching-up conversation and then finally, Risa got right into the instruction:

"Oren, from what we currently know and understand about the mind and its structure is that the mind arises through the paring of consciousness and matter. We know there are three forms of awareness.

"The mind brings forth *Perspective Awareness* which allows you to perceive the world around you. Then we have *Reflective Awareness* which allows you to look within yourself to know the inner cosmos. Reflective Awareness and Perspective Awareness emerge out of the original form of awareness which we call *Resonant Awareness*. Resonant Awareness allows a person to acquire information through sympathetic resonance. It allows us to know through *feeling*.

Perspective Awareness is a function of the *Mind*.

Reflective Awareness is a function of the *Soul*.

Resonant Awareness is a function of the *Spirit*.

"What comes along with Perspective Awareness, to form the mind, is a whole host of psychic elements and dimensions of reality including, our perception of the world, imagination, fantasy, personality, thoughts, emotions, instincts, fear, delusions, ego defense mechanisms, and so on.

"The mind arises out of a collision between consciousness and matter. All the elements of the mind I just mentioned, arise out of this collision in a fractured semi-coherent state. It's imperfect.

"The Human Soul, also called the Noetic Soul, True Self, and Authentic-Self, arises in the mind trying to see through and work past all the psychological elements of the mind.

"It's very easy for the Authentic-Self to get lost in the jungle of the mind and lose itself among all the automatic programs which compete with the Authentic-Self for control over the mind.

"The discipline I am about to share with you is a way for you to draw-out your Authentic-Self, recognize all the parts of your mind and integrate them into a unified mind as you liberate your true self.

"The mind is born incomplete. The Noetic Soul (Authentic-Self) has the innate power to rise up within the mind to integrate it and complete it if it so chooses.

"This indicates that the mind must become self-aware for it to become complete. Many people never stand up to complete the process. Instead, they just allow their automatic response reflexes and ego defense mechanisms to rule their mind.

"If we live our entire life this way, we die incomplete and are compelled to reincarnate over and over again until we finally wake up and complete the integration process to unify the mind," says Risa.

Oren interjects and responds, "This is fascinating information. Do you know why we are compelled into this process?" Risa answers:

"Our body of scientific knowledge, although vast, does not know all the answers yet. We do know there is a dichotomy between consciousness and matter, and together they give rise to the mind.

"We also know that the rise of the Human Soul (Noetic Soul, Authentic-Self) within the mind has the ability to unify it all.

"We're also able to track the reincarnation of the Human Soul through our quantum resonance technology. We know the Human Soul has the innate power to transcend the reincarnation process, if in its prior existence, it unified the mind. Again, we don't know why yet. We just see the results. We know this much scientifically. But we still have many unanswered questions," says Risa.

Oren responds, "How can someone actually guide him or herself through this process? It just seems so complicated."

Risa answers, "Actually, the human being does not guide the process, the process guides itself through a law in the universe called the *Law of Sympathetic Resonance.* The force of operation within this law is called, *Alpha.* Alpha is the manifestation of the law itself.

"The moment someone starts applying his or her own conscious awareness upon his or her own mind to integrate it, Alpha begins rising within them to guide the process.

"Alpha brings forward what you need to see and integrate next. You just remain still and become aware of all the elements.

"Alpha even starts directing the course of your life to bring about what you need to discover next," explains Risa.

Oren responds, "Wow, I feel like I just woke up, but also like I want to go back to sleep again. This is overwhelming."

Oren chuckles a bit but then continues asking questions:

"Where does Alpha even come from?" asks Oren.

"Great question," replies Risa.

"We can only make a hypothesis based on our observation of the force itself. What we know is that Alpha is the self-organizing force of the universe. We also know that Alpha is not part of creation. Rather, it counteracts creation and is trying to steer it and guide it. It keeps reorganizing creation to a higher reality. It's moving everything toward something. It appears to be trying to reunify everything from where it originally came forth," says Risa.

"From where did everything come forth?" asks Oren.

Risa responds:

"We don't know yet. We're all in this together trying to figure it out. We are sharing with you what we know so far and what we don't know. Other people keep coming along to study the same mystery and sometimes they find a missing puzzle piece. Maybe through the course of your life, you will find a missing puzzle piece and share it with the rest of us," says Risa.

"Okay. So how do I do this discipline? How do I compel Alpha to rise within me to unify my mind?" asks Oren.

"Alpha is already moving through all things in the universe right now. What we know is that Alpha will speed up its momentum within a person in response to the intercession of a *conscious mind*.

"What's important is not what we would consider a conscious mind, but what Alpha would consider a conscious mind. We know what Alpha considers a conscious mind by how it responds to and measures what a mind does. There are three basic things that when a mind is doing them, Alpha says, "Aha!" this mind is conscious, or is becoming conscious, and starts accelerating its momentum within it. We call these three things, *The Three Factors*," says Risa.

"Fascinating, what are these Three Factors?" asks Oren. Risa responds and explains:

First Factor: "The First Factor is the mind observing and measuring itself with the intent to transform and integrate itself. We practice the First Factor with meditation and self-observation techniques which I will begin sharing with you today.

Second Factor: "The Second Factor supports the First and Third Factors by neutralizing all your psychic and biomechanical energy to keep your mind clear, so your conscious mind is able to discern all its constituent parts. There are many Second Factor exercises. They all involve some form of movement where we are mixing and neutralizing our energy with either the energies found in our environment, the energy found deep within ourselves, or the energies found in other human beings. Human beings can neutralize each other's energies. Martial Arts is a practice of the Second Factor.

Third Factor: "The Third Factor is Love. It is through Love that we compel the transformation and integration of our minds. What we know is that Love is a force which arises when Awareness becomes aware of its own Life. Awareness, Life, and Love form the trinity of our ultimate reality. This trinity underlies everything in the universe. We cannot explain how it is what it is. We just know it's there. We know it's there because we can work with them to integrate the mind. Traditions call this underlying Love in the universe, *the Spirit*. Love is the Spirit of Life. The Spirit is what gives rise to energy and movement. The Third Factor develops our relationship with the Spirit. We utilize the force of the Spirit in the meditation practices of the First Factor to transform and integrate the mind. The Spirit is the agent of transformation.

"The Second Factor helps us to reach the Spirit. The Spirit is magnetic neutral in energy, versus magnetic positive, or magnetic negative. This is why, in the Second Factor, we are seeking to neutralize our energy. By neutralizing our psychic and biomechanical energies, our conscious mind is able to make a super cognitive-emotional connection with the Spirit. Once this higher emotional connection is made, we can then utilize the Spirit in the First Factor to transform and integrate the mind. All three factors work together. The Third Factor is the most important of the three factors.

"When Alpha detects a person working with all Three Factors, Alpha begins accelerating its momentum within the person to integrate his or her mind," says Risa.

"So essentially, a conscious mind is a mind working consciously with the Three Factors," says Oren, in a confirming statement.

"Yes, exactly, this is what Alpha is telling us by its response to the Three Factors. You learn quickly, Oren. I like that," says Risa.

Raiden decides to chime in:

"Oren, I have been practicing the Three Factors since the same age as you are now. It helps me do everything better. It brings harmony to my life. It underlies everything I do, yet it's invisible to everyone. No one sees me doing it.

"The Three Factors reflect the natural behavior of a conscious mind. It's what the mind does when it is conscious of itself and the universe. The universe responds to it, and in return, guides it along its journey. This is *Alpha*," says Raiden.

"The First Factor is *Transformation*.

"The Second Factor is *Cultivation*. The Third Factor is *Love*. "You see, it's all quite simple," adds Raiden.

Risa continues: "Oren, the first thing that you need to do is split your mind into the observer and observed. When you start looking inward by using your *Reflective Awareness,* you can begin discerning the many constituent parts of your mind.

"Eventually, you will discover the universal force of the Spirit. When connecting with the Spirit, we utilize *Resonant Awareness*. Your internal reflective awareness reconnects your conscious mind to the source awareness, which is Resonant Awareness.

"The force of the Spirit is extremely powerful. Once you have gained the cognitive ability to feel and know all the parts of your mind, you can contrast your awareness of the Spirit against these parts of your mind, and when you do, these parts will transform. When an element of your mind transforms, a dimension of your true self is liberated, and your mind becomes more unified.

"The practice of contrasting the Spirit against an element of your mind you are trying to transform, is called *Differential Resonance*. Anything you bring into Differential Resonance with the Spirit will transform. What causes the actual transformation during a moment of Differential Resonance is the force of Alpha.

"What causes us to become aware of all the parts of our mind we need to transform, is the adversity of life. We use all the challenges of our daily lives to bring about the opportunities to transform. If you are transforming yourself amid all your life challenges, you will transcend them and become the master of your own existence," says Risa.

"I am speechless. How do I do this?" asks Oren. Risa answers: "I'm giving you general instruction now, but your Dad already knows how to do the actual practice. You will work with him each day until you get a handle on the practice. The practice itself is very easy. What's hard, is life. We are giving you a set of tools to transcend yourself amid all your life challenges.

"There are many ways to observe yourself; one such way is through what we call, *The Five Centers*. Some approaches focus on the energy within the organs of the physical body. However, the system I'm sharing with you utilizes the five centers.

"The five centers correspond to distinct functions of your mind. In the transformation practice, we focus on a mood, or state of mind, which is causing us some form of pain, stress, or discomfort. We breakdown this mood and understand it by observing its nature within the five different centers.

❖ CHAPTER THREE ❖

"One of the laws of transformation is that you first must truly comprehend the nature of what it is you are trying to transform before it will transform. To reach the appropriate level of comprehension, the understanding cannot be analytical, intellectual, or even contextual. It must be a higher emotional understanding.

"We need to extract the understanding out of our feelings. It must be a super empathic understanding. The understanding emerges without deduction or logic. It's actually the faculties of the mind such as deduction, rationality, and logic, which makes something subjective. The understanding arises spontaneously beyond the mind. There is no process to it. You stay focused on the element until the understanding arises. The comprehension transcends the mind.

"You keep moving your focus of awareness between each center experiencing the mood of the psychological element in that center. Stay in each center of the mind for a few minutes and then switch to another center of the mind. Experience the feeling of the mood in the (1) *emotional center* (heart area), then switch to (2) *the mental center* (in your head) and feel that same mood in the mental center, then switch to (3) *the instinctive center* (in your abdomen). Stay in the instinctive center for a few minutes and then switch back to the emotional center. Go deep inside the feeling.

"You will notice how the same psychological element has a different expression in each of the five centers of the mind.

"It's okay to keep reliving the life experience in your mind during the meditation practice to provoke the particular mood to rise in the mind to keep working with it. You need to feel it to work with it.

"Keep stirring up that mood with your memories so you can go deeper into the feeling.

"The other two centers are your (4*) motor center* between your shoulder blades, and (5) in your *sexual center* in your genitals. In the motor center, we experience how the psychological element makes us move. In the sexual center, we can feel how the psychological element steals energy, or how it stirs energy.

"There are also superior centers beyond the five centers. It's in the superior centers that we experience the Spirit.

"After you have a really good higher emotional understanding which exceeds your language ability to express it in words, then start praying to the Spirit for that psychological element to transform.

"Don't imagine or project what the element should transform into. Allow the transformation to happen on its own. You will first feel the psychological element getting lighter and softer in feeling. When it starts getting lighter, start searching for a new understanding of what the psychological element is transforming into.

"Allow the new understanding to arise on its own. What eventually emerges, is a new aspect or dimension of your Authentic-Self.

"The new aspect of your Authentic-Self will have an even quality of energy among all five centers. It will be the same in each center. This is how we know the difference between what is *false* and what is *authentic* within us. What is false, fractured, or unintegrated will have a different expression in each of the five centers. What is authentic will have an even and uniform quality among all five centers.

"When most people first start this practice, while praying to the Spirit, they don't feel the Spirit with their emotions. They feel nothing. This is normal. They're praying in the dark, so to speak.

"The goal is to eventually reach the Spirit where you can feel the Spirit with your emotions. At that point, you can contrast your feeling of the Spirit with your feeling of the psychological element you are trying to transform. It's at this point you are bringing the targeted psychological element into Differential Resonance with the Spirit. It's at this point that you will start experiencing a rapid and profound transformation of each psychological element," says Risa.

Oren interjects and asks, "How do I reach the Spirit?"

Risa explains: "By practicing the Second and Third Factors we reach the Spirit. Your work with Third Factor will bring forth the Spirit while you are working in a practice of the First Factor.

"Any practice which facilitates and cultivates true love or causes one to transcend oneself and go beyond oneself, is a legitimate practice of the Third Factor. Learn to love other human beings. Listen to music which stimulates your higher emotions. Learn to forgive. Strive to be authentic every day," says Risa.

Raiden chimes in:

"There is also another way. Sometimes the Spirit is reaching out to us. It reaches out to us through our dreams and our visions. Have you ever had a dream, or a vision, where, for a brief minute, you felt something extraordinary, something divine, or an exquisite higher emotion?

"Some people have experienced this in a near-death experience. They cannot describe it. This is the Spirit," says Raiden.

"Ah! I understand now," says Oren.

Risa chimes back in:

"Great! Oren. Use whatever you're remembering of the Spirit in your First Factor transformation practice.

"Invoke this feeling you're remembering of the Spirit while you are focusing on a psychological element and bring them both into Differential Resonance. I promise you, if you keep doing this, it will transform," says Risa.

All three sat for some time while Oren sat with his eyes closed explaining what he was feeling within each of the five centers while going inside different memories of his life to re-experience the moods associated with those memories.

Risa instructed Oren that while he is going about the day, to keep self-observing his feelings in the emotional, mental, and instinctive centers, and then later in the day, when he could sit and meditate, to go back to the moments of the day when he caught something which he wanted to study. At this point, he should study the psychological element in all five centers, one center at a time.

"Okay, that's enough for today, Oren. Let's meet again in three days. Between now and then, please keep a journal of all your self-observations and retrospective practices. When you and I meet next, we will discuss your journal and your inner experiences," says Risa.

"Great! Thank you so much, Risa! I already feel different just learning all this. It is very enlightening. I have a lot to think about," says Oren.

They give their courtesy good-byes and farewells to each other. Raiden and Oren are now making their way back home.

CHAPTER FOUR

THE OMICRON ORDER

While en route back to the villa, Raiden receives a call from *Special Agent Kira Gyson* informing him that the intelligence team is ready to give a debrief on Scorpius. They will meet at the Center for Foreign Intelligence (CFI) in two hours. King Sah and Lord Giao join Lord Raiden at the CFI building inside a special operations room.

About 20 high-ranking military and special intelligence officers are in the room. Special Agent Kira Gyson is standing in front of the room to conduct the introductory segment of the special intelligence briefing. Kira begins speaking:

"Good afternoon King Sah, Lord Raiden, Lord Giao and members of the intelligence team. As you already know, there is an advanced human race living in the Messier 4 (M4) globular cluster in the constellation of Scorpius. The M4 cluster is actually far beyond the main stars of Scorpius but is still in the Scorpius constellation.

"The M4 cluster is about 5,200 gamma (6,500 Earth light-years) beyond Antares, the brightest star in Scorpius," says Kira.

One gamma is how far light travels in one Orion year. One Orion year equals 1.25 Earth years. (5,200 Gamma x 1.25 = 6,500 ELY) Kira continues: "On the Anthronex Scale, the Scorpius humanity is a type 1.5. It has already colonized multiple planets in multiple star systems throughout its stellar neighborhood. Their government is a republic, thus, its name, the Scorpius Republic. The home-world of the republic is the Planet *Serapas*, the fifth planet circling the star *Kronos* in the M4 globular cluster.

"Kronos is the central star in a triple-star system. The two stars orbiting Kronos are *Hyperion* and *Theax*.

"Only 12 years ago (Orion years), Hyperion underwent a massive stellar novae event. It blew off its outer shell. Hyperion is only a half a gamma from Kronos.

"About 30 years before the event, the Scorpius Republic became aware that Hyperion was about to go stellar nova in a relatively short period of time and decided to act quickly. They declared martial law and placed General Cyrus Urlex in charge until all populations were safely relocated. It was handled systemically in military fashion.

"All civilian populations were evacuated to planets a safe distance away or were sent further inside their home-worlds to seek shelter. Serapas evacuated all populations on its surface to either off-world or to its already very extensive deep underground cities.

"The agreed timeline was that martial law would remain in effect on all worlds in the republic until the equivalent of 10 years after Hyperion went stellar nova and then General Urlex would hand back power to the elected government. It's been 12 years. It has become clear that General Urlex has no intention of handing back power to the elected government. All planets in the Scorpius Republic remain under martial law.

"We decided to take a closer look at General Cyrus Urlex. We initially discovered he was a member of a secret society called the *Omicron Order*. We now believe he is their leader. The discovery of the Omicron Order's involvement in Scorpius is why we called this special intelligence session today. The Omicron Order arose 100,000 years ago and was thought to have been vanquished 20,000 years ago. All that happened is they moved underground to become a secret society with a hidden network across many star systems.

"The Omicron Order has a religion based upon genetic engineering. Their goal is to bring about a new race of *metahumans*. The Omicron Order believes all *non-genetically enhanced* humans to be inferior and that a superior intelligence must intervene with the spontaneous process of creation to direct the course of evolution to ensure the improvement, proliferation, and continuity of the species.

❖ THE OMICRON ORDER ❖

"The goal of the Omicron Order is to refashion the human species on all known planets by constantly cross-breeding metahumans with non-metahumans. They're doing this at higher and higher intervals. They operate in secret across their vast network.

"The star systems they have been targeting for the past 20,000 years are star systems hosting human civilizations existing somewhere between type 0.25 and type 1.5 on the Anthronex Scale. The humanity in Scorpius is type 1.5. The Orion Empire is type 2.0. The Omicron Order itself considers the metahumans in charge of their Order to be functioning on par with a type 2.25 civilization.

"The Omicron Order is entering a new phase of its operation where they will reorganize all star systems in the M4 globular cluster into their home star group. Scorpius M4 will become their central plexus of galactic operations.

"They will not stop there. They will continue their effort to impose their genetic program on all other humanities. Eventually, they will target the Orion Empire itself.

"The Omicron Order saw the stellar novae event coming long before the republic. They were secretly positioning themselves. They were waiting for the crisis to arise to exploit it and take power.

"General Cyrus Urlex himself was genetically designed to become a new military leader in the Omicron Order. He is the product of all their top geneticists coming together to create the most intelligent and strongest human being they could possibly engineer.

"The problem is, we don't know the full extent of their existence. They could be billions of people by now. Most people involved in their genetic program would not even know they're a part of it. We don't know the full extent of their reach into legitimate organizations, economies, and governments all across the galaxy. They may have already entered the star systems of the Orion Empire.

"There's one more thing. Evidence indicates that the more genetically enhanced a mind becomes, the more it loses its empathy. It becomes psychopathic.

"The human mind has two spheres which must maintain a delicate balance. The two spheres are the *Noetic* and the *Erotic*.

"On the noetic side, we have will, conscious choice, self-awareness, realization, contemplation, reflection, empathy, and critical thinking.

"On the erotic side, we have our animal instincts, fight-or-flight, fear, desire, ego defenses, automation, computation, and programming.

"If the noetic side doesn't rise up to assert its own light of consciousness, the erotic side will rise up automatically and overrun the mind with its own programmed instinctive nature and become the governing authority of the mind.

"The noetic side of the mind is what makes a person human. The erotic side is run by the soul of creation which runs through and animates all living creatures. Everything which is automated and programmed by nature emerges from the erotic sphere of the mind.

"The noetic sphere must balance the erotic sphere. Both are needed, but there must be a balance between them both.

"The problem with genetically enhancing the mind is that, the only side which can be genetically enhanced is the erotic side. The erotic side can be programmed. The noetic side cannot be.

"The erotic side is where the computer of the mind is located. It's where all the automated programming of nature occurs. The more you enhance the programs of the mind, the more you tilt the balance of power toward the erotic side, and the more the noetic side is suppressed. The more you enhance the computer side of the mind, the more psychopathic the mind becomes overall," says Kira.

Raiden chimes in:

"The genetic enhancement of the mind is a form of dark alchemy. The only way to upgrade the mind is through an intentional awakening. We upgrade the mind by integrating, not by genetically enhancing. The noetic side must lead the process."

Lord Giao interjects:

"Kira, so what you are telling us is that we have a human race of genetically enhanced, extremely intelligent, super strong, psychopaths, running around the universe with all the military and financial resources of the Scorpius Republic? Is that correct?"

"Yes, Sir. That is what we are telling you, Sir," answers Kira.

Lord Giao continues:

"And to make things worse, these psychopathic metahumans are spreading like a virus by cross-breeding with other non-metahumans. They're spreading their psychopathy like it's a disease," says Giao.

King Sah speaks:

"We need to be extremely careful here. This is not a war which can be fought and won with starships and the military alone.

"If we act too quickly with force, we could bring this disease into the Orion Empire even faster," says King Sah.

"Father, you are very wise, and I understand your point of view. However, I think we need to go in and bite the head off the snake before it takes over the Scorpius system," says Lord Raiden.

Lord Giao responds to Raiden:

"Raiden, let's stop and think about this. Let's not be too impulsive. We need to be very strategic. Right now, we are not involved, but the moment we get involved, there may be no way out," says Lord Giao.

"I think I should take a special commando unit and take out the leadership of the Omicron Order. We will lie low. They will not see us coming or going. They will never know it was the Orion Empire," says Lord Raiden. King Sah chimes back in:

"Raiden, you just came home from a two-year military mission. You need to stay home and recharge. Your family needs you. The Omicron Order has been around for 100,000 years. We're not going to end it with one decapitation strike. This will only rattle the Scorpion and drag ourselves into a situation we cannot get out. Let's spend some time gathering more intelligence," says King Sah.

Meanwhile, in Scorpius, the military is beginning to split due to the ongoing disagreement between General Cyrus Urlex and the elected government of Scorpius. Many senior officers seem conflicted in their loyalties. Many are strongly standing behind General Cyrus Urlex, while the other senior officers are strongly on the side of the elected government under *General Mason Holloway.*

General Holloway has a massive fleet of ships amassing inside several hollowed-out rocky moons orbiting the gas giant, *Mabbas,* the furthest gas giant orbiting the nearby star *Verazon.* The hollowed moons are now functioning as giant space hangars.

The President of the Scorpius Republic, *Quinten Meir*, is riding aboard a military shuttle taking a tour of the Scorpion fleet. General Mason Holloway is standing next to him on the bridge of the shuttle. They're approaching one of the Mabbas moons. They start making their way toward a large crater situated just beyond a rocky mountain range. The four quadrants of the crater floor begin slowly pulling backward revealing the inside of the hollowed-out moon.

As they make their way toward the inside of the Mabbas moon, it's a sight to behold. Thousands of ships are parked and lined up both horizontally and vertically in a three-dimensional matrix pattern.

The Scorpion ships look very different from the Orion ships. The Orion ships have a purity of form and function. The Scorpion ships are not so conservative. The design of the Scorpion ships sacrificed agility, speed, and group formation tactics, for overwhelming firepower.

However, this Scorpion fleet under General Mason Holloway is not getting ready for a battle with the Orion military, they're getting ready for battle with another Scorpion fleet under General Cyrus Urlex.

"General Holloway, do we have any advantages we can count on in our fight against General Urlex and his forces?" asks Quinten Meir.

"General Urlex is woefully underestimating the size of our force. Due to his personality profile, degree of political influence, and strength of his command over the forces he leads, about 20 years ago we began thinking we could have a problem with General Urlex," says Mason. (1.00 Scorpion year = 0.90 Orion years.) Mason continues:

"In response, we opened *Sector 99*, a secret space program within the military-industrial-complex commissioned to build starships out of sight of the elected government. This was done in case we had to forcefully take back power. To keep it a secret from General Urlex, we also kept it a secret from you and all elected officials," says Mason.

Quentin looks over at Mason with a serious face.

"This is very troubling Mason, but under the circumstances, I'm glad we have the ships. However, this could be a self-fulfilling prophecy. If we keep thinking a certain outcome will arise, there will be an unconscious provocation within us to manifest that outcome. We have to be equally conscious of our adversary, and ourselves," says Quinten.

"You are a very wise man, Quinten. The goal here is not to destroy the opposing forces but to get them to stand down. After all, they're still our own brothers and sisters.

"Quinten, look off to your left. This is our new Galaxy Class Destroyer, *The Antares*. It is the most powerful ship we've ever built. General Urlex has no idea of its existence. It's two generations ahead of its time. When they first see the Antares, they will run like hell! They will be in total shock and awe," says Mason.

Quinten turns to his left and looks.

"Holy S%#t! Wow! OMG, it's extraordinary! It's massive!" says Quentin as he gazes upon the imposing galaxy-class destroyer.

The Antares is glowing an iridescent blue. It has large extending wings stretching out and down on either side of the hull of the ship. Huge laser cannons are mounted beneath the wings on each side of the ship. There are no visible engines. Like the Orion ships, the Scorpion ships utilize gravity propulsion. The wings themselves are not wings. They're part of the hull of the ship. Within the wing structures are 15 crew decks. You can see their windows lining the wings providing much more front and rear side visibility.

Meanwhile, on Serapas, home-world to the Scorpius Republic, and quickly becoming the Scorpion Empire, General Cyrus Urlex is seated upon what almost looks like a throne, but in actuality, is just a chair mounted on an elevated platform giving him a better view of the instruments all around him. He is casually holding up and reading a tactical report on a high-tech see-through device while five officers are approaching him. Behind General Urlex is a vast array of screens displaying various logistical maps of the stars which keep moving and adjusting in real-time.

General Urlex is extremely fit and tall. He was made as best the scientists could make him. He is the product of the most advanced genetic engineering of his day. His mind, however, is more computer-like than human. He lacks empathy and any ingratiating social skills, most of which he finds annoying and a complete waste of time. It shows in his personality. His personality is brash, stoic, superior, condescending, combative, and self-important – a classic sociopath.

❖ CHAPTER FOUR ❖

He can put on his charm when he needs to, but it's all an act. He leads through fear and intimidation because he really doesn't know any other way to feel or be. His mind, however, is a machine. He is brilliant, calculating, and ruthless. He will stop at nothing to accomplish his goal. His biggest weakness is his delusional sense of self. It's hard for him to take advice from others. Mostly, he just likes others who validate his views or follow his directions without debate. What's odd is that, despite all his brilliance, he can't see himself in a mirror. Most people can see there's something not quite right with him, but he actually thinks he has everyone fooled.

Somehow humanity always seems to let people like this take power. We subconsciously admire their veracity and tenaciousness. We feel as though it's making up for something missing inside us. We like them until we realize, it's too late.

The persona of a narcissistic sociopath is the *Mark of the Beast*. Due to its appealing attributes, many people in the modern world subconsciously recognize it, copy it, and seek to buy and trade by it. What people should really seek within others, and within themselves, is *Authenticity*. Authenticity is the greatest quality a person can have.

You can have every trait a person could wish for, but if you lack authenticity, then you actually have nothing. If you have authenticity and nothing else, then, in actuality, you already have everything.

General Cyrus Urlex talks to the officers as they walk up to him. "Do you have an update on the whereabouts of President Meir?"

"Yes, Sir. He was last seen with General Mason Holloway, but we lost track of them after they crossed the plaza and entered the shielded domain of the Serapas military headquarters. They could be anywhere by now," says *Commander Amelia Varen*.

General Urlex pauses and is thinking to himself.

"Bring in *Commander Garrett Cartrite*," says General Urlex. Commander Cartrite walks in a few minutes later.

"General, what can I do for you, Sir?" asks Garrett.

"Commander, please arrange for a meeting on the *Grid* tonight. All senior officers are required to attend," says General Urlex.

"Will do, Sir," says Garrett.

Garrett leaves General Urlex and heads back to his office to begin making arrangements for the senior officer meeting later that evening. On the way, he sees his good friend and newly promoted senior officer of the Omicron Order, *Alexander Wolf.*

"Hey Alex, can you walk with me on my way back to my office?" asks Garrett.

"Oh, hey Garrett, yes, sure."

Alex drops what he is doing and begins walking with Garrett.

"Alex, tonight, we have a meeting on the Grid," says Garrett.

"The Grid? What's that?" asks Alex. They're now walking outside together between buildings in the underground world of Serapas.

"Only senior officers of the Omicron Order know of it and utilize it, and since you only just became a senior officer last week, you have not yet been informed of its existence," says Garrett.

"Okay, what is it?" pressed Alex.

"The Grid is a virtual reality construct used to hold senior leadership meetings of the Omicron Order. No one has ever been able to figure out how we all meet and coordinate. We are very hidden. We never meet physically. We only meet on the Grid. The Grid is non-local. It instantly connects all of us across vast distances of space."

"How does it work Garrett? Do we put on some kind of headgear where we see and talk to each other remotely?" asks Alex.

"Actually, it's much more sophisticated than that. The foundation of the virtual reality construct is built upon a naturally-occurring neurosynaptic grid found latent at the quantum level of the universe. The neurosynaptic grid forms a *neuronet* connecting all minds of all lifeforms on an unconscious level across the universe. Most humanities do not even know of its existence and we hope it stays that way.

"The Omicron Order developed a special *cyberoptic technology* to utilize the neuronet carrier wave operating within the neurosynaptic grid, also called the *interlink frequency*, as a backbone to run our virtual reality construct. There are many advantages to using the neuronet as the underlying backbone.

"Number one, it's naturally occurring. We don't have to build the underlying network or architecture. It's already there.

"Number two, the energy required to run the program is extracted out of the neuronet itself. It supplies an unlimited source of low-voltage energy, perfect for running a virtual reality program.

"Number three, no one can detect it because it's not artificial. We run an artificial program through it, but the neuronet itself is natural.

"The computer software interfaces with and utilizes the neuronet and together they create the virtual reality construct. It's a combined synergy between the two sources, one natural, and the other artificial.

"There is a dimension of the virtual reality construct derived from real information arising from all the minds of the interlinked participants. It makes the virtual construct more real," explains Garrett.

"This is absolutely fascinating. How does a person enter the Grid and utilize it?" asks Alex.

"A person enters the Grid during sleep with the use of a *neural cortical node*. The cortical node causes the body to fall asleep while forcing the conscious mind to stay awake in a lucid self-aware state. The cortical node synchronizes the frequency of the conscious mind with the frequency of the virtual reality construct. This allows the conscious mind to enter the virtual reality construct and function inside it. We each have an avatar body while inside the virtual reality construct. The avatar body is our virtual body. It carries forth our conscious mind.

"Another advantage of this technology is that, to enter the virtual reality construct, all you need to do is go to sleep with a cortical node. The cortical node can be hand-held, worn around your arm, or even embedded inside your body. We have calcium-based cortical nodes now. The calcium cortical node is placed inside your leg bone. It cannot be detected. The calcium-based cortical node is masked by the calcium inside the bone. The cortical node is programmed to respond to certain thought patterns of your own choosing in order to activate it. This makes the technology completely hidden," explains Garrett.

"This is extraordinary. Where does the computer running the program reside?" asks Alex.

"No one knows this. Only General Cyrus Urlex would know this. This information is passed on from one leader of the Omicron Order to the next. Only the leader knows this kind of information," says Garrett.

"Wait. How old is the Grid?" asks Alex.

"It's been around a long time. At least since the time the Omicron Order went underground 18,000 years ago," says Garrett. (1.00 Scorpion year = 0.90 Orion years).

"Alex, in three hours, go to the laboratory of *Dr. Liam Zhou*. He will give you a cortical node and sync it with your brain. He will help you with your first session and monitor your progress," says Garrett.

"Yes, Sir," says Alex.

Three hours later, Alex arrives at Dr. Zhou's lab. Alex walks into the lab where one of his assistants greets him.

"Hello, what I can do for you?" asks the assistant.

"I was sent here to see Dr. Liam Zhou. Commander Garrett Cartrite sent me to see him," says Alex.

"Okay, please wait here for a few minutes and I will see if I can find him. He's most likely in his lab," says the assistant.

A few minutes later Dr. Zhou walks into the room.

"Hello, I am Dr, Zhou. How can I help you?" asks Dr. Zhou.

Alex responds:

"Dr. Zhou, Commander Garrett Cartrite sent me to your laboratory to see you," says Alex.

Alex then reaches over and whispers in Dr. Zhou's ear:

"Garrett sent me to see you about a cortical node," says Alex.

"Ah yes, you must be Alex," says Dr. Zhou.

"Yes, Sir, I'm Alexander Wolf, very nice to meet you," says Alex.

Dr. Zhou smiles and shakes Alex's hand.

"Good to meet you Alex. I've been expecting you. I have everything already prepared in the lab. Your meeting on the Grid starts in 30 minutes. We need to move quickly. Come this way," says Dr. Zhou.

They proceed through a special security area. Dr. Zhou's lab has the highest level of security clearance. The Grid is a tightly-kept secret. All of Dr. Zhou's work involves the Grid and the interfacing of the human mind within the virtual reality construct. It was actually Dr. Zhou who invented the calcium-based cortical node. They walk down a corridor and then into a small room. Once the door is closed behind them, Dr. Zhou spins a bookcase leading into a corridor of a secret area.

They walk down the corridor and turn right into a special room with a reclining chair and technical instruments all around. There are two lab assistants in the room getting ready to prep Alex.

"Mr. Wolf, we need you to change your clothes," says one of the lab assistants as she hands him some light loose-fitting clothes.

"We will be hooking-up various monitoring sensors to you. These clothes will make it easier," says the first lab assistant.

"Okay," says Alex, as he steps into a small room to change.

Alex is now changed and ready. He is sitting and waiting while one of the lab assistants is working on a computer and the other is drawing blood from Alex.

Dr. Zhou says to Alex: "Garrett told me he already gave you a debrief of the Grid and what it is. I think the best way to find out, is to just enter it. Have no concern. We have been doing this for a very long time. The virtual construct, and the science behind it all, is very advanced and refined. You are in good hands. You will see Garrett and all the senior officers in a few minutes," says Dr. Zhou.

One of the lab assistants is placing sensors on Alex's head and body. "Alex, we are hooking up sensors to sync your new cortical node to both your brain and to the interlink frequency of the virtual construct. We're giving you a calcium cortical node but this time we will just fasten it to your body with an arm wrap. If you wish, we can embed it in your leg bone at a later date," says the first lab assistant.

"Alex, we need you to lay back and relax and just breathe normally and try to quiet your mind. When you feel your mind is quiet, please let us know," says the first lab assistant.

After a couple of minutes of breathing, Alex says:
"Okay, my mind is quiet."

The second lab assistant says: "Alex, this next step is important. We're going to program your cortical node with your own thought command. We need you to think of a word and then repeat that word over and over again in your mind. In the future, when you say this word in your mind, it will activate your cortical node. Your cortical node will only respond to your inner voice when saying this word."

"Alex, do you have a word?" asks the second lab assistant.

"Yes, I have a word," says Alex.

The word Alex is thinking of is the word "Carbon."
He just saw the word on the periodic table of elements hanging on the wall in the laboratory. It stood out to him.

"Okay, now start saying your chosen word very clearly in your mind and keep repeating it. Do this for one minute - starting now," says the second lab assistant.

While Alex is saying his word quietly in his mind, the two lab assistants and Dr. Zhou are closely watching a neural monitor. After about 30 seconds the neural monitor signals that it has successfully recorded Alex's thought command.

Dr. Zhou walks over to Alex to explain what happens next.

"Alex, your cortical node now has your chosen thought command. We also have your neural wave pattern. In just another minute your cortical node will be ready to take your conscious mind onto the Grid while your physical body is sleeping. The computer is taking a moment to sync your neural wave pattern with the interlink frequency hosting the virtual reality construct," explains Dr. Zhou.

Alex is listening and thinking while lying on his back.

"Wait, I have a couple of questions. How do I come back? And how long will this first session last?" asks Alex.

"When you're ready to come back - just think it. Something else you can do is pinch your hand with your thumb while you're inside the virtual reality construct. The first session will last only one hour. We will let you wake up naturally but if you do not wake up within an hour then we will wake you up ourselves," says Dr. Zhou.

"Okay, sounds good. I'm ready," says Alex.
Dr. Zhou says: "Alex, let's begin. Keep your eyes closed and pretend like you are falling asleep. Focus on your breathing. Say your command word in your mind. Every couple of seconds repeat your command word in your mind."

Alex feels himself drifting off to sleep while repeating his command word. Suddenly, he finds himself fully conscious walking toward some old gothic style mansion in the late midnight hour.
The scene looks like Medieval Europe in the 1300s (14th century).

❖ CHAPTER FOUR ❖

Torches and pine trees are lining the pathway to the mansion. Alex looks down to see himself dressed in 14th-century dress clothing. Interestingly, this time period is actually way off in the distant future on the faraway planet we call *Earth*.

The virtual reality software extracts information out of the neurosynaptic grid underlying the entire universe and renders the information it gathers as part of the virtual environment.

The information the software picks up is both non-local in space and non-linear in time. The programmers gave a degree of freedom to the software to render what the artificial intelligence governing the program determines to be meaningful or appropriate in some way. In this case, the program is picking up and incorporating random information arising out of the Grid regarding 14th-century Europe on Earth in the far-off future.

The scientists who developed this program say it's actually the Grid itself proposing the information to render. The software is just listening to the Grid. This points to a dimension of mind embedded within nature itself. This is not a common virtual reality program. The program is cooperating with a cosmic anomaly. Perhaps it's just the universe organizing and reflecting our own collective intelligence.

Alex approaches the mansion. He sees strange gargoyles adorning the building. For a minute, it even seems like the gargoyles are moving and looking at him. The front entrance is ominous. He walks up the steps of the mansion and knocks on the front door. The door opens.

It's Garrett! He has a smile on his face as he welcomes Alex through the front door. Alex is walking into the mansion bewildered. Standing in the large front foyer of the old mansion are many senior officers of the Omicron order.

"So, what do you think Alex, is this cool or what?" asks Garrett.

Alex responds: "This is unbelievable! This feels more like some kind of lucid out-of-body experience! Are we all going to remember the same experience when we wake up?" asks Alex.

"Absolutely, a matter fact, each person's cortical node records their experience. We can play it all back later and compare notes. If you forget something about the meeting, you can always go back to it on your computer or even re-immerse yourself in the experience and review the session. However, sessions marked secret, such as this one, are never recorded. All Omicron meetings are always secret. Once inside the hall, all recordings will stop." says Garrett.

"This is getting more and more extraordinary," says Alex.

All the officers in the grand foyer are talking and catching up with each other when there is a call to gather in the mansion's meeting hall. The crowd begins filing inward. Alex decides to follow the crowd.

They all enter a large opera hall with seating organized in tiers surrounding a podium. There must be 4,000 senior officers in the hall. Alex is amazed to see how many senior officers there are of the Omicron Order. It was a much larger organization than he realized.

Everyone is seated while General Urlex makes his way to the podium. Everyone is dressed in 14th-century clothing such as were worn in the royal courts of Europe. Fourteenth-century Europe is millions of years in the future 6,000 light-years away. The General begins speaking:

"Good evening senior officers. Tonight, all senior officers of the Omicron Order were called to this assembly. We are at the threshold of our next transformation which will bring about a new era and a new higher level of existence for all humanity. All of us here today have sworn a solemn duty to carry out and fulfill what needs to be done to achieve our destiny. Our destiny is to become a superior human race. To become the best that we can become. Evolution is not our master. We are destined to be our own masters of our own evolution.

"All of you here today are the founders of a new age in which we will accomplish new and extraordinary things. The work each of you is doing will be remembered throughout history," says the General.

The crowd shouts out in unison and says, "HAIL OMICRON!" General Urlex continues speaking:

"General Mason Holloway has no idea of our level of infiltration into the forces which he thinks he commands. We have allowed his illusion of control to persist while he digs himself ever deeper into our trap. He thinks we do not know of Sector 99. He thinks we do not know of the new fleet of starships they've been building and hiding inside the Mabbas moons of the Verazon star system.

"We have been allowing him to build our new fleet for us. Let them do all the work and then we will come and harvest the fruit. Soon we will take control of our new fleet of starships."

"I called you all here today to remind you to remain steadfast in our cause. Everything is proceeding exactly according to plan. You all have been given your own mission to carry out when you are given the secret command. That command will come like a thief in the night.

"At that point we will strike a fatal blow at the heart of the enemy. That day is coming soon. It is upon us. I will not say when I will give this order. It will be received by all of you simultaneously via your cortical nodes. You all know the secret command words you will hear me speak. When you hear it, you must immediately carry out your task with fervent and unflinching resolve. If any of you have not yet embedded your calcium cortical nodes, you must do so immediately. Your cortical nodes must now be carried with you at all times unseen and undetected by everyone around you," says the General.

The crowd shouts out again in unison saying, "HAIL OMICRON!" The General continues speaking:

"We are all brothers and sisters fighting for a cause much greater than ourselves. We all deeply believe in what we are doing. We know this cause will elevate the human existence for all of humanity.

"My dear brothers and sisters, please enjoy the rest of your evening here in our beautiful mansion. I encourage each of you to say hello to any new or unfamiliar faces and get to know one another. You are all family," says General Urlex.

After saying these final words, General Urlex leaves the podium. All the officers stand up and begin fraternizing and socializing.

Alex is less interested in meeting the other officers and more interested in looking around the mansion.

He decides to take a stroll. He leaves the opera hall and begins walking down a corridor. At the end of the corridor, Alex sees a pair of glass doors leading outside. He walks outside to a garden area. He's amazed by the virtual environment. If someone woke up in this virtual environment, they would never know it wasn't real. A person could not distinguish this virtual reality environment from actual physical life.

Everything here feels physical. All five senses are working perfectly. The environment mimics the same natural laws of physics. Everything, down to the smallest details, is accurate; even the subtle outdoor smell of the trees; the smell of the fire torches; the sounds of the crickets; the touch of the velvet of Alex's vest; the small cracks in the stones of the garden walkway. Nothing is left to one's imagination.

Alex is walking through a garden behind the mansion late at night. It's very eerie. He can hear the nighttime sounds of the animals.

No other person is around. He sees a path with an archway covered with ivy. He looks down the pathway to see pitch blackness. His heart is thumping. He's thinking, "man this is creepy."

He decides to venture into the darkness. As he's walking down the dark path, he looks toward the ground to the right of him and sees a pair of yellow eyes staring up at him from within the weeds. He makes eye contact and the eyes disappear.

"Wow, what the hell was that?" he's thinking to himself.

He reassures himself that this is only a virtual reality construct and nothing bad is going to happen to him. He decides to venture further.

He looks up and standing about 15 feet in front of him is something which scares the hell out of him. It's a tall slender apparition of a powerful-looking woman dressed in glistening black skin-tight clothes with a black crown on her head and a snake entwining and moving along her body. She looks up at him with a pair of large cat eyes. He looks back at her in total shock and fear.

Alex immediately turns around and starts walking away quickly. He stops near a tree and pinches his thumb to wake up.

Alex wakes up in the reclining chair in Dr. Zhou's lab. Dr. Zhou and his two assistants are in the room. Dr. Zhou says:

"Welcome back Alex, how was your first meeting?"
Alex is looking all around him. He still can't get the image of the scary woman out of his head, but he decides not to mention it.

"It was extraordinary, Dr. Zhou. I am completely amazed by how real it all was. Of course, I cannot talk about the meeting itself.

"Dr. Zhou, can we schedule the implantation of my cortical node?" asks Alex.

"Yes, come back tomorrow afternoon and we will do the implantation," says Dr. Zhou.

They finish-up and Alex expresses his gratitude to the doctor and his two assistants and says he will be back tomorrow afternoon.

The next morning Alex meets up with Garrett for breakfast.

While eating, they're comparing notes about the meeting on the Grid the night before. Sure enough, everything matched. Alex reconfirmed everything General Cyrus Urlex had spoken. Towards the end of their conversation, Alex decides to share with Garrett his experience in the garden behind the mansion. Garrett responds:

"Alex, you just met and came face to face with *the Gorgon*. She is a powerful ally of the Omicron Order. She is our *Oracle*."

"What? She's an Oracle? We have an Oracle? Is she human?" asks Alex. Garrett responds:

"Actually Alex, we are not quite sure what she is. She manifests right out of the Grid itself. It's not part of the program. The virtual reality construct has many strange anomalies we cannot control. These anomalies arise out of the organic side of the virtual construct. They arise out of the naturally occurring neurosynaptic grid," says Garrett.

"When the program first went online, the scientists tried to weed out these anomalies, but we have since learned to embrace them and work with them. These anomalies are all pointing to something. They're trying to tell us something. The fact that you saw this in your first session means something, but I don't know what. You will find out what it all means as time goes by," says Garrett.

Let's now rewind and go back to the evening before.

After the senior officer meeting at the mansion, General Urlex is the last one remaining in the Omicron mansion. He decides to take the opportunity while all alone to go visit the Oracle.

He heads outside to the garden behind the mansion. He stops at the outside patio separating the garden and the mansion.

The General looks up at the sky for a minute to see all the stars. He sees a full moon with clouds racing over the face of the moon. He can hear the sound of coyotes howling in the distance. The General smiles at the moon and then begins walking toward the garden path.

He's walking down the garden pathway and passes underneath the ivy archway and down the same trail Alex had gone down earlier in the same evening except General Urlex goes much farther.

Now past the point Alex had gone, General Urlex passes between two large oak trees forming an entrance to a dark abode.

Just beyond the pair of oak trees is a small stone Greek-style temple. The General walks fearlessly straight for the temple.

Approaching the temple, he walks slowly and then stops to gaze upon the steps and what lies beyond. Out of respect for the temple he takes a moment to place his mind in a quiet and solemn state before entering.

After pausing for a minute, the General enters the temple and slowly walks past the colonnade to come upon a stone altar burning with fire.

Beyond the altar is an elevated chancel.

A throne chair sits high upon the chancel overseeing the altar of fire. Along either side of the throne are columns with snakes descending. General Urlex kneels in devotion to the Oracle and says:
"Oh, Queen of the night, please come forth and give me guidance."

The General looks up to see the Gorgon, the Omicron Oracle, sitting high upon her throne.

"My dear Cyrus, why have you come here today?
"What will you do for me to make me want to do anything for you?" asks the Gorgon Queen in her wicked narcissistic voice.

General Urlex is bent down on one knee with his head down. "My dear Queen, I will do anything you ask of me. All I ask in return is for your guidance in our effort to defeat President Quinten Meir and General Mason Holloway," says the General.

"Cyrus, we have spoken of the prophecy of the Dark Lord who will eventually rise up to lead the Omicron Order.

"I request that when the day arrives for me to tell you who the Dark Lord is, that you seek out this person and make him the leader of the Omicron Order," says the Gorgon Queen.

"I swear an oath to fulfill your request my dear Queen," says Cyrus.

"Very well, Cyrus, my power will be with you in your fight with General Holloway. Wait for Holloway to make the first move. Lay low until then. Wait until he fires the first shot," says the Gorgon Queen.

CHAPTER FIVE

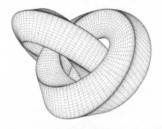

THE GAMES OF OLYMPIA

Back in the Orion Empire, Raiden is enjoying time with his family. It is only on the rare occasion that everyone is home at the same time and the royal family is taking advantage of it. Usually, at least one or two members of the family are off-world on some form of official duty.

They're visiting concert halls, royal balls, waterparks, horseback riding, family picnics, sporting events, and outdoor games. Raiden and Giao even have a chance for a sparring match at the dojo.

The sparring match gets everyone's attention. Giao himself trained alongside Raiden in martial arts while growing up. Compared to a human on Earth, Giao is only nine months older than Raiden.

Word travels fast through the village that Raiden and Giao are about to spar at the village dojo. In a short time, a crowd is forming trying to catch a view. Raiden and Giao notice the crowd and decide to take their match outdoors so everyone can see.

The match shows an extraordinary set of skills from both. Neither can land that strong a blow against the other. It looks more like a choreographed dance than an actual fight. Giao is more on the offensive. He's trying to figure out how to get past Raiden's defenses. Each is bending like a reed in the wind against the other's attack and each of their attacks is perfectly timed and executed. You can see they are both getting a real workout from each other. No one else in the village could stand toe-to-toe with Raiden. Oren is no match yet for his uncle, Lord Giao. The crowd watches in amazement.

After about 15 minutes, Raiden and Giao stop, turn, and bow to the crowd. Everyone erupts in applause. There was no clear winner; however, Raiden had more speed and he executed his moves more smoothly and accurately. Giao was more out of breath and very happy the match was finally over.

That evening, Raiden and Giao sit down for a game of chess. Giao says to Raiden:

"My brother, you won our match today at the dojo, but now you're in my dojo, although I did get in a couple of good shots."

"You did great Giao. I was very impressed. I haven't had such a good workout in a while. It's been some time since I've played chess so please go easy on me," says Raiden.

"Not a chance! Your older brother is about to teach his younger brother a big lesson!" says Giao. They both laughed.

The Royal Families of the Bellatrix Dynasty are known to be quite modest. They've captured the hearts and minds of all their people.

They don't live in a palace. They live in a royal villa surrounded by a village. Although, they do have a monarchy, beneath that monarchy, is a Democratic Republic with an elected Prime Minister. The current Prime Minister of the Orion Empire is *Bernadette Rigel.*

In the Orion Constitution there is a balance of power between the elected government and the monarchy. The Prime Minister and the elected government manage the internal affairs of the Orion Empire. The monarchy manages all foreign affairs, the military, and the Supreme Court of Justice.

Also, in the Orion Constitution, there exists what are called *Super-Entities.* A super-entity is any organization which has become so strong and influential within society that it can power-broker and shift the outcome of public policy. Super-entities are limited in their influence by the Orion Constitution just like the elected government.

Super-entities must adhere to special restrictions, guidelines, and responsibilities to protect the people from the potential tyrannical influences of the powerful, yet unelected. A company with a monopoly would be a super-entity but under the Orion Constitution, a super-entity is not limited to only companies with a monopoly.

❖ CHAPTER FIVE ❖

In the Orion Empire, the media, unions, organized religions, banks, corporations, academia, and big social media companies, would all qualify as super-entities. Super-entities are not considered part of the government, but they are held to a higher standard of responsibility toward the general public.

Super-entities are recognized as social entities which have the power to do great good but can also do great harm. This is all to protect the power and self-determination of the individual. It's not to protect the power and self-determination of those in power. The freedom of the individual is paramount.

Out of profound respect for the freedom of the people, the monarchy keeps a low public profile. It is only on special occasions that the royal family appears together in an official manner. One such special occasion, which has become customary, is the *Olympic Games*.

The tradition of the Olympic Games began with the Orion Empire. It was picked up much later and copied by the Greeks.

The Olympic Games are traditionally held every four years in the Orion Empire on a planet within the Bellatrix star system but outside of the protected Erawan domain. Erawan is the third terrestrial planet orbiting Bellatrix. The Olympic Games are played on the seventh terrestrial planet orbiting Bellatrix called *Olympia*.

The words *Olympia, Olympian,* and *Olympic* come from the word *Olympus*. The word *Olympus* is a proto-Greek word meaning *Mountain or Sky*. The word *Olympia* means "*of Olympus*," otherwise meaning "*of mountains and sky*." Olympia was actually much more than just a place in Greece where the Olympic Games were played. Olympia was originally a *planet* where the Olympic Games were played millions of years ago. The Greeks copied this tradition in honor of the Orion people who they considered to be gods.

Olympia was also more than just a planet for sporting events. Olympia was a galactic planet where the Orion Senate was located as well as many embassies of other star systems throughout the galaxy. Most of the Orion government buildings were on Olympia. They were not on the Orion home-world of Erawan. Erawan was too sacred and private to be hosting the forums of government.

❖ THE GAMES OF OLYMPIA ❖

The forums of government were purposely not located at the center of the Orion Empire. Government was seen as a necessity, but not as a central need for the lives of the Orion people. The off-center location of the government was a reminder of that principle to both the Orion people and to those serving in government. The actual power was with the people of Erawan, the true center of the Orion Empire.

Olympia is a water world with unusually high mountain ranges. The mountains touch the sky. The water is clear, still, and serene. There are no waves because there are no moons orbiting Olympia.

Planet Olympia is composed of a mysterious combination of Himalayan-like mountains emerging out of Caribbean-like Oceans. About two-thirds of Olympia is water. Olympia would be considered a Super-Earth. Its diameter is twice that of the Earth.

Olympia has one ancient city on the surface. The age of this city is over two million years old in Orion years. It is the capital city of Olympia. To date, this city has managed to survive all natural catastrophes and is historically preserved out of reverence to the Orion ancestors who built the city. The name of the city is *Arcadia*.

Like the word *Olympus*, the word *Arcadia* is originally Orion. Arcadia is a majestic capital city with super-tall crystalline towers. The towers absorb all the energy needed from the Bellatrix star. They were built with memory materials possessing self-healing properties. Android ships with a sentient artificial intelligence built the towers through a super-advanced injection mold process. They stand several miles high.

The capital city from afar looks like a large collection of giant white crystal shards rising high into the sky.

The royal family is making a trip from Erawan to Olympia for the official start of the Olympic Games. They all meet out on the plaza where Raiden and Kizor Bayzor had arrived a few weeks prior. As a security measure, King Sah, Lord Raiden, and Lord Giao never travel together in the same vessel.

Three shuttles are waiting for them. The ships are light and feathery looking. They have a minimalist purity of form and function.

King Sah and Queen Adoriti are in one shuttle. Lord Raiden, Princess Chae, Prince Oren, and Lady Aria Solis are in the second shuttle. Lord Giao and Desa Maggis are in the third shuttle.

All three shuttles lift off quietly hovering for a minute motionless in the air, and then like the wind taking dandelions in the breeze, they begin gliding swiftly through the air in complete silence.

The shuttles are flying through the sunlit cavern paradise like birds flying toward the sun.

The lake water is sparkling below them while the lush green land wraps mysteriously upward on either side of the underground world.

They're flying into beams of sunlight penetrating the morning mist in front of them.

The shuttles fly just beyond a set of undulating green hills to make a sharp turn upward into a dark void above.

It's dark for only a moment until the darkness turns into an expansive city space filled with fast-moving aerial vehicles coming and going. City lights and little ships light up the darkness of the void.

The three shuttles are now floating upwards, slowly spinning into a bright column of light.

They follow the light until the shuttles emerge from the inside of the planet into the Erawan atmosphere. Below the shuttles, there is a pristine landscape of pink, lavender, touches of green, and a majestic blue body of water beyond.

They're above the Erawan north pole. The shuttles make another sharp arc upwards toward space and within seconds they're beyond the Erawan atmosphere.

In front of them is a large space station. The station has taken a remote hold of the shuttles. They're being guided toward a docking bay. A few of minutes later, the shuttles are setting down inside the station. Like all other people, the royal family adheres to the rules and changes shuttles at the station. There's a greeting party awaiting the royal family. The royal family is escorted to a different hangar bay where there are three more shuttles of a different but larger design.

These shuttles are interplanetary. They're designed to travel only between the various celestial bodies of the Bellatrix Star System.

The three interplanetary shuttles quietly rise and begin hovering inside the docking bay. Then, like taken by a light breeze, the shuttles move gracefully into space. Waiting for the shuttles is a fleet of small-size warships ready to escort the shuttles to Olympia. The warships surround the group of shuttles in a V configuration.

A second V configuration of warships follows behind.

The ships begin moving quickly. Within minutes they arrive at the Erawan stargate. As customary, all other ships awaiting passage on both sides of the stargate line up in formation for the royal procession. The fleet quickly makes its way through the gate.

Once beyond the Erawan gate, the ships in the fleet synchronize their resonance to act as one, and then suddenly, they all vanish. Typically, Orion ships don't warp into an uncontrolled area of space but because the Orion forces are already in control of the space surrounding the destination, the ships fold space on their way to the nearby planet. The fleet reappears a short distance from Olympia.

Like Erawan, Olympia has a security field enveloping the entire planet. However, the shuttles don't need to dock at an orbiting station.

All visiting ships are directed to enter through either the north or south pole and they must land either at the stations below each pole or at the capital city of Arcadia.

The royal fleet is headed for the south pole. The entire fleet enters the atmosphere together making its way to Arcadia which is situated halfway between the south pole and the equator along the shore of the largest continent. The fleet is hugging the shoreline just above the water cruising alongside a jagged mountain range as they approach the capital city of Arcadia.

The giant crystal city of Arcadia appears ahead on the horizon. The fleet lifts higher into the air as they approach the ancient city. The crystal towers are sparkling in the sunlight as the royal fleet approaches. All other air traffic has been steered away or grounded while the royal family makes their approach. The shuttles land on a landing platform at the top of one of the tallest towers in the city. A greeting party is awaiting the royal family, including Prime Minster Bernadette Rigel.

The members of the royal family exit their shuttles and are approaching the greeting party. King Sah and Queen Adoriti are at the front. Prime Minister Bernadette Rigel speaks:

"Your Majesty, your Highness, members of the royal family, we are honored by your visit today. Welcome to Olympia. We have a wonderful series of events planned for this year's Olympic Games."

Queen Adoriti responds:

"Bernadette, thank you. We are all very happy to be here today. We're looking forward to the events and to seeing everyone over the next three days."

King Sah chimes in:

"Bernadette, thank you. It's great to see you again. I received your message the other day. Lord Giao and I will make some time tomorrow to discuss your ideas. Please make the arrangements."

The royal family rests inside the tower penthouse to prepare for the forthcoming activities. Later that evening, it's the opening ceremony to the official Olympic Games. The royal family is seated inside a giant colosseum in their special area overlooking the crowd. The architecture looks remarkably familiar. Orion architecture is the forerunner to Greek, Roman, Egyptian, and Babylonian architecture.

The Orion Empire sought to emulate what they saw as a universal geometry of form, symmetry, and balance. They pioneered the study of sacred geometry.

King Sah and Queen Adoriti are seated in the middle. To the King's immediate right is Lord Raiden. To the Queen's immediate left is Lord Giao. To the right of Lord Raiden is Princess Chae, Prince Oren, and Lady Aria Solis. To the left of Lord Giao is his concubine Desa Maggis and Prime Minister Bernadette Rigel.

The master of ceremonies (MC) is making introductions. He finally introduces the royal family and says:

"Ladies and Gentlemen, with us here this evening, it is my great honor to present the royal family of the Orion Empire."

A spotlight shines upon the royal family as they all stand and wave. They're all being televised on giant TV screens positioned along the top perimeter of the colosseum for the entire crowd to see.

❖ THE GAMES OF OLYMPIA ❖

This event is being broadcast across hundreds of star systems of the Orion Empire. Each star system in the Orion Empire has its greatest athletes competing in the Olympic Games.

The MC continues speaking about the royal family and says, "We have our most revered and venerable majesty, King Sah."

The king is waving as the whole crowd erupts in thunderous applause with whistles and cheers. The Orion people adore King Sah. They already believe him to be one of the greatest kings in the history of the Orion Empire.

The MC continues: "We have our beloved Queen Adoriti."

The crowd continues cheering and whistling as the queen waves.

The MC continues and says:

"And we have our most brilliant Chief Justice, Lord Giao."

The crowd is cheering and whistling.

Then the master of ceremonies says:

"And of course, we have the great Lord Raiden, Supreme Commander of the armed forces, heir to the Orion Empire, and our next King."

The crowd goes absolutely berserk!

They love Lord Raiden!

They know all about his military conquests and acts of chivalry! The master of ceremonies is trying to settle the crowd but cannot.

The crowd is chanting:

"Raiden! Raiden! Raiden! Raiden! Raiden!"

You can see how proud the whole royal family is of Raiden as he receives huge praise from the crowd. Princess Chae and Prince Oren are wiping tears away as the people continue chanting:

"Raiden! Raiden! Raiden! Raiden!"

King Sah puts his arm around his son, Raiden. He lifts Raiden's arm high into the air as a confirmation that Raiden will be the next King.

The only people who don't look so pleased are Lord Giao and Desa Maggis. Lord Giao is holding back his anger and faking a smile. He is barely clapping his hands. Desa is watching Giao with concern on her face. Both Giao and Desa remember they're being watched and regain their composure and continue clapping for the crowd.

Shortly after, Lord Giao stands up and excuses himself and goes inside the suite. He's checking some of his messages, but you can see his mind is still bothered by what he just witnessed.

Desa goes inside. She places her hand on Giao and says:

"Giao, I'm sorry, I know that must have bothered you."

Giao responds:

"It's okay, Desa. It's about time I start facing reality. Raiden will be the next King. My father kept me closer by his side all my life. I thought perhaps he was priming me for the throne. Obviously, I was mistaken. It doesn't really matter. I'm still the Chief Justice of the Orion Empire."

He turns and looks at Desa sternly in the eyes and says:

"I am the law."

After the opening ceremonies, the crowd gets to watch the first sporting event of the Olympic Games known as *Hoverball*.

The game is played on a racetrack.

Each player stands on a floating disk. They can move in any direction by the way they tilt the disk with their feet.

If you tilt the disk downward toward the front, the disk will move you forward.

If you tilt the disk to one side, it will move you to that side. If you tilt the backside, the disk slows down.

The more the disk is tilted, the faster it goes in the tilted direction. The more you tilt the backside, the harder it brakes. The players must have excellent balance otherwise they will fall.

The racetrack is a traditional oval with 14 lanes.

At either end of the track, at the tip of each oval, is a small goal hovering above the lanes.

The objective of the game is to move the ball forward and score as many shots on goal as possible within the time allowed. There are three 30-minute times periods.

The ball is passed between team members while trying to avoid the opposing team as they race toward the goal. The opposing team tries to steal the ball away and speed ahead to the opposite goal.

❖ THE GAMES OF OLYMPIA ❖

Each team has their own goal to defend. The game always moves counter-clockwise. It never changes direction.

The players are allowed to knock each other off the hover disks. Everyone wears protective gear. If a player takes a shot on goal and misses, then the player just sent the ball flying in the direction of their own goal which helps the opposing team.

The ball has a three-second timer. A player can hold the ball for only three seconds before having to pass it or make a shot on goal. If a player holds the ball too long, the ball will become slippery and will automatically move. It instantly rises and goes backward for another player to catch it and take charge of the ball.

Each team has seven players for a total of 14 players on the track. There is one player per lane. Players can switch lanes only when holding the ball. There are no goalies. The ball can bounce on the track, but it cannot go off the track; otherwise, the other team automatically takes possession. Each player must stay in his or her lane except to check another player with the ball or if the player is holding the ball. If it's to check another player with the ball, they must immediately return to their lane after checking the other player. If they miss the check, this is considered a foul and the player's disk will automatically take the player off the track for 2 minutes.

The game starts with all the players lined up in an alternating pattern. When the whistle blows, the ball shoots up out of the track and everyone tries to catch it - and the game begins.

Coincidently, the Scorpius Republic is the reigning Olympic champion in Hoverball. Their greatest player is *Rexus Kahn.*

The Orion Empire invites other star systems to the Olympic Games who are not part of the Orion Empire. It's a great opportunity for trade talks and intergalactic diplomacy. Not every star system has athletes good enough for the Orion Olympics, but every four years, in Orion years, new star systems usually join the games.

The first game of Hoverball is between Scorpius and Betelgeuse. The Scorpius team is wearing black and silver uniforms with blue helmets. The Betelgeuse team is wearing purple and white uniforms with yellow helmets. The hoverboards match the helmets in color.

❖ CHAPTER FIVE ❖

The President of the Scorpius Republic, Quinten Meir, is at the Olympic Games. Quinten Meir reached out to Bernadette Rigel hoping she could arrange a meeting with King Sah.

Bernadette is not aware of the Omicron Order and the latest developments in Scorpius.

Bernadette gets up from her seat to see Lord Giao inside the suite. "Giao, as I already mentioned, Quinten Meir would like to see your father. He just sent me another message asking if he could stop by our suite and see you all. Is this okay?" asks Bernadette.

"Yes, of course, this is a good idea. Please arrange for Quinten to see us immediately," answers Giao.

A short while later, President Quinten Meir and his entourage arrive at the royal family's suite where they're about to watch the hoverball match between Scorpius and Betelgeuse.

It should be a great game. Betelgeuse has a terrific team. After 20 minutes of pleasantries, Lord Raiden, Lord Giao, and King Sah step into a private room with Quinten.

"Gentlemen, thank you for seeing me today. I ask that our conversation stays only among us," says Quinten.

"Of course," says King Sah. Quinten continues speaking:

"As you know, the Scorpius Republic has been managing through a major crisis due to the star, Hyperion, going stellar nova. We've been under martial law for the equivalent of 12 Orion years, but it was only supposed to have lasted 10 Orion years. We are undergoing an insurrection by General Urlex.

"We believe he is a threat to other systems, not just to the systems belonging to Scorpius. He will eventually become a problem for the Orion Empire. The elected government of Scorpius is willing to align itself with the Orion Empire if you are willing to help us," says Quinten.

King Sah responds:

"Quinten, we are also aware of the fact that General Urlex is the leader of the Omicron Order and that it is really the Omicron Order who is leading the insurrection. The problem is the way they're organized. They have sleeper cells everywhere. This is not purely a military problem. They're spreading their genetic program like a virus."

Standing next to Quinten is his head of central intelligence, *Director Heinrich Kezrich*. Director Kezrich says:

"There's actually a deeper unseen dimension to the problem. We happen to know that the Omicron leadership meet and coordinate within a virtual reality construct they call the *Grid*. To date, we have not been able to access their virtual construct. We do have three of their cortical nodes which they use to access the Grid. Our scientists and engineers have not been able to penetrate them to figure out how they work. Perhaps you have people who can analyze one of them?"

Heinrich reaches in and takes a cortical node out of his pocket. He has an ominous look in his eyes as he reaches over and hands Giao the cortical node.

The moment Giao takes hold of it, he hears the sound of clamoring voices - like voices coming through an old transistor radio.

While hearing these voices, Giao has a waking vision of the garden behind the Omicron mansion. He sees the two large oak trees and the dark abode beyond. Giao snaps himself out of it and says:

"Thank you, Director Kezrich. Our people will take a look at it."

Giao hands the cortical node to Raiden. Raiden is also in charge of the ministries of science and medicine. Raiden places the cortical node in his pocket.

King Sah responds:

"We want to help you Quinten, but we fear our involvement will only drag us into a civil war and a larger problem we cannot escape."

"Your Majesty, you're already in deeper than you realize. The Omicron Order is everywhere. The sooner you start responding to it, the sooner you will get on top of it," says Quinten.

"Quinten let's move slowly. We will continue to engage through diplomacy and provide you with any technical support that we can. This is not an Orion military matter. Please stay in contact with Giao. In the meantime, we will analyze the cortical node," says King Sah.

Raiden chimes in while pointing to the game:

"Shall we all go watch the game together?"

They all agree and head toward their seats overlooking the event. It's about to start. They're introducing the players.

❖ CHAPTER FIVE ❖

As they announce the players, the players are gliding upon their hoverboards around the track waving at the crowd. When they get to Rexus Kahn, he's making a muscle pose on his hoverboard with his arms curled in the air.

As his hoverboard glides past the royal family and their guests, Rexus is pumping his fist. The crowd is going crazy. Quentin lifts his fist in the air in a show of support for Rexus.

The royal family and their guests stay for the entire game. It's a very exciting match. No one knows this, but the Scorpius team is made up of all metahumans. The game is a demonstration of their superior strength and athleticism.

Raiden takes keen notice. You cannot see much of a reaction from Quinten but Director Kezrich seems especially proud of the Scorpius players. He cheers Rexus and keeps an eye on the royal family's reactions to the Scorpius team's skills.

The Scorpius team wins the game 12 to 10.

The next morning, Raiden and Giao make their way to a neuro-cybernetic specialist on Olympia, *Dr. Mira Owenshaw.*

They're in a shuttle flying from one side of the capital city of Arcadia to the other. They're speeding and weaving around the tall crystalline towers.

Thousands of craft are coming and going in different directions. When looking down there are multiple tiers of skyway traffic. The buildings are so tall you can't see the ground. All the craft land at different building floor levels within the towers lining up with the multiple tiers of skyway traffic.

While en route Giao shares something with his brother Raiden. "Raiden, last night when Director Kezrich handed me the cortical node, it affected my mind somehow," says Giao.

"Really? What happened?" asks Raiden.
He tells Raiden that he heard voices and had a vision of a pair of trees with a strange dark abode beyond and then he snapped out of it.

They approach one of the towers and land softly inside one of the tower's docking bays.

CHAPTER SIX

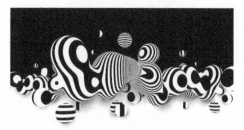

INTO DARKNESS

R aiden and Giao are walking to Dr. Mira Owenshaw's laboratory. As they arrive, and after some initial pleasantries, they get right to the point. "Mira, we received something last night we need you to analyze," says Raiden as he hands her the cortical node.

"It's a neuro cortical node which provides the conscious mind of a person user-access to a virtual reality construct. We need you to find out as much as you can about it," says Raiden.

Giao interjects to say something.

"Mira, something strange and unusual happened to me last night when I briefly held the cortical node. I heard voices - and I had a strange waking vision," says Giao.

"Very interesting. We will definitely analyze it. What was your vision, Your Majesty, if you don't mind me asking?" asks Mira.

Giao retells his experience to Mira.

"Okay, we will take a look at it immediately. How long will you be on Olympia?" asks Mira.

"We will be here another two days," answers Giao.

"I only ask because I may want to run a couple of tests while you hold the cortical node," explains Mira.

"Understood, please contact either me or my brother when you know something or if you wish me to come back," says Giao.

Sure enough, the next day, Dr. Mira Owenshaw reaches out to Raiden and Giao via a video call.

"Lord Raiden and Lord Giao, thank you for taking my call.

The cortical node is extremely advanced in that its technology is completely organic, yet it operates inorganically as a cybernetic device. There is nothing synthetic about its chemical composition.

"What's interesting, however, is that the organic structure of the molecules in the cortical node is re-configured and re-arranged to operate as a circuitry.

"Most people would think the cortical node is just a bone fragment. It's made up of the same chemistry found in a human leg bone. The major minerals of the intercellular composite are calcium and phosphate. It's very possible that no two cortical nodes will have the same configurations. We also ran various brain waves through the cortical node. Based on what we see, we believe the cortical node is meant to be used during sleep," explains Mira.

"Mira, very interesting! What should we do next? asks Raiden.
Mira responds:

"What we would like to do next is have Lord Giao go to sleep while holding the cortical node. We would like to do this in my lab so we can monitor the entire process.

"Giao, would you be willing to do this?" asks Mira?

"Hold on! Is there any risk to this?" asks Raiden.
"We don't believe so, but there is no way for us to know for sure until we try it. The cortical node is completely organic. We don't believe there is much risk," says Mira.

"What if this is some kind of mind-reading device and this is just an attempt to steal information out of Giao's mind?" asks Raiden.

"Actually, we can monitor if there is any outflow or downloading of information and if there is, we will immediately interrupt the process and wake Giao up from his sleep," says Mira.

Giao interjects: "I'm willing to do it. I'm very curious and would like to try it. Are you okay with this Raiden?" asks Giao.

"I'm willing to go along with this, but I want our best experts in the room and if there is any downloading going on, it has to be immediately interrupted," says Raiden.

Late that evening, Lord Giao heads back to Mira's lab to undergo the sleep experiment with the cortical node.

Giao is in the lab with Mira and one of her assistants. Several secret service agents are observing everything to make sure Giao remains safe. The royal family's private physician is with them supervising. The secret service agents and the physician will intervene if they become concerned with what they're witnessing.

Mira explains to Giao how they plan to proceed:

"Lord Giao, the cortical node is based on an organic technology. In order for it to work, the cortical node and the neural frequency of your conscious mind must enter into harmonic resonance.

"Certainly, the engineers behind this technology have a computer system which synchronizes the user's neural pattern with the cortical node and the underlying frequency of the virtual reality construct. We don't have their computer system to do this, but we can improvise.

"Based on your experience in holding the cortical node, it seems there's already a level of naturally-occurring resonance between you and the cortical node. We're going to tune into that naturally-occurring resonance and amplify your neural connection with the cortical node. In other words, we're going to hack into the program.

"The first step is to discover the interlink frequency which carries and supports the resonance between your conscious mind and the cortical node. We will place monitors on both you and the cortical node to tap into and discover the interlink frequency.

"To establish the initial connection, we will have you perform a retrospective memory exercise to bring back the same psychic state you had when you first held the cortical node which triggered the vision.

"We need you to feel the same and think the same.

"If a new waking vision arises, we ask that you raise your hand. This will help us to pinpoint the interlink frequency," says Mira.

While Mira is saying all this, Giao is reflecting upon what he was feeling at the moment he took hold of the cortical node.

He was feeling anger.

He was angry over the crowd cheering for Raiden and his father raising Raiden's arm to confirm he would be the next King. It's easy to bring back that anger because he's actually still angry.

For Giao to re-enter the same dark abode he saw in his waking vision - he will have to re-enter the same dark place within himself.

"Okay, I understand. This makes perfect sense," says Giao.
Mira continues speaking.

"As we isolate the interlink frequency and your internal psychic state, which last night triggered the connection with the cortical node, we will implant a mental command between you and the cortical node to serve in place of a triggering-psychic-state.

"It's easier to make a mental command than it is to bring back a psychic state to re-enter the virtual reality construct," says Mira.

"Got it. I'm ready," says Giao
Mira continues speaking:

"Before we start, we need to think of a mental command to function as a trigger between you and the cortical node. This will make it easier the next time you try to enter the virtual construct," says Mira.
Giao interjects:

"What kind of command, like a word or a phrase?" asks Giao.
Mira explains.

"It should be a word. This type of virtual reality construct is well-written and theorized about in cybernetic journals but, to date, no one has ever declared to have actually invented one. In the cybernetic world it's called, *"Neuronetic VR."* Obviously, someone already invented it and has been keeping it a secret.

"The command word is a prescribed step in the theoretical process. The user is supposed to think of a special command word. The word needs to be a short one or two-syllable word which is very sharp and clear in your mind. You say it only inside your mind, never aloud. The user keeps the command word a secret," says Mira.

"Ah! Okay. I have a word," says Giao
The word Giao is thinking is *Barstow*. Barstow is one of the two sacred moons of Planet Erawan. The twin moon of *Barstow* is *Jenesis*.

Both moons are about the size of the Planet Mercury. They each support an exotic ecosystem of life. The lifeforms on these two moons still possess some extremely rare qualities of the first lifeforms which crossed-over from the primordial universe to the physical universe.

The moons are considered primordial sanctuaries and are forbidden to everyone. There has to be a special reason to visit them and the visits must be approved by King Sah himself. The moons have an extraordinary sacred power to regenerate and restore life.

Lord Giao is laying down face up on a medical bed in the lab. Mira strapped the cortical node to his upper arm.

Various neural monitoring sensors are hooked up to both Giao's head and cortical node. The lab assistant is injecting a mild sedative into Giao's arm. Mira address Giao:

"Lord Giao, we are now tracking two wave patterns on our computer screens. One wave pattern is associated with your conscious mind and the other wave pattern is associated with the cortical node. We're watching for a harmonic convergence between the two wave patterns. This will be the interlink frequency.

"Please recall the state of mind you had when you first held the cortical node in your hand. If you can, correlate any prior events with your state of mind in that moment, and then retrospectively go back to those same events and relive them in your mind," says Mira.

Giao follows Mira's instructions and has no trouble bringing back his earlier state of mind.

"I'm there Mira. I now have the same feelings and thoughts of yesterday evening," says Giao.

Giao has mixed feelings of anger, fear, rejection, and ambition. He fears the future. He fears not having power. He fears humiliation. He feels rejected by his father. He has an insatiable ambition to prove his greatness and to be accepted. His mind is sinking into darkness.

"Very good! Now start repeating your command word in your mind. Tell both your mind, and the cortical node, that the command word represents your desire to enter the virtual construct," says Mira.

Giao is resting quietly. There's some suspense in the room while everyone watches. After a few minutes, the monitors start flashing. There's a harmonic convergence of wave patterns on the screen.

Mira starts typing quickly. She's isolating the interlink frequency supporting the convergence between the wave patterns. She has it! Now she's stabilizing and amplifying the neural connection.

Mira looks over at Giao. He has rapid eye movement indicating he has entered REM sleep. She's surprised at how quickly he fell asleep.

The cortical node is actually designed to help the user enter sleep while directing the user's conscious mind into the virtual reality construct. Mira does not know this.

Mira quickly checks all Giao's vitals and other biometrics and everything is fine. The royal physician is in agreement. Everything checks out. The royal physician signals to the secret service agents that everything is okay. They seem relieved.

Meanwhile, Giao's awareness has been taken onto the Grid. His mind is sliding down a dark tunnel as if going down a slide.

Suddenly Giao finds himself walking behind the Omicron Mansion. He's amazed at where he's at. He feels completely awake and alert. It all seems physical. He remembers that his body is in Mira's lab and that this is the Omicron virtual reality construct.

He looks down at his body. It's a mirror image of his physical body yet he's dressed in strange clothing. Giao is dressed in 14th-century medieval European attire.

He's looking around. It's late in the evening. No one is around. The crickets are singing. A full moon is lighting the path before him. Giao looks to his right and sees the big gothic mansion. Bats are flying around the eves and dormers of the roof. The gargoyles look menacing.

As he begins walking, there's a light scent in the air coming from the trees, shrubbery, and burning firewood off in a distance. He's looking around. Giao stops to see the ivy archway on the left.

The archway and its dark abode beyond are beckoning him forward as he stares at it from afar. He feels the dark path calling out to him, but it feels too ominous. He's more interested in following the moonlit path as he continues walking. There's a sound of metal hitting metal up ahead. As he walks, the sound is getting louder and louder.

Up ahead there is a faint orange glow coming from a small shed. Ah, it's a blacksmith hitting a piece of hot iron over an anvil with his hammer. "Hello there," says Giao to the blacksmith.

There's a universal translator embedded in the Grid. You hear and see your own native language when hearing or reading any words.

"What brings you to these parts of the woods late at night? Don't you know you shouldn't be walking around here this late in the evening?" asks the blacksmith.

"I'm sorry, I'm a bit lost, but it's nice to meet you, Sir," says Giao.

"This is no place to be getting lost, son. There are people who've wondered these parts and never been seen again," says the blacksmith.

"Why? What can you tell me about this place? What goes on around here?" asks Giao.

"That mansion up ahead is the Omicron Order headquarters. It's purposely located in the deepest part of the forest far away from the rest of the world. God only knows what really goes on inside there, but people are always going missing around here.

"Not too far from here is the temple of the Gorgon. She's a local legend. She's known as the *Queen of the Night* because at night she roams the local area.

"Trust me, you don't want to run into her," says the blacksmith.

"Wow, that's really strange," says Giao.

"Strange indeed, but she's no myth. She's for real. I've seen her more than once myself," says the blacksmith.

"What do you know about her?" asks Giao.

"The Omicron Order worships her. They see her as some form of a supernatural deity. She's their Oracle. She guides them and in return they do her bidding," says the blacksmith.

Giao is not scared to hear all this because in his mind this is all just a virtual reality construct. How could any harm possibly come to him?

He's thinking he needs to meet this Gorgon Oracle so he can learn more about the Omicron Order. This is an opportunity to gather critical intelligence. He doesn't want to squander it. This opportunity may never come again.

"Where would I go to find this Queen of the Night?" asks Giao.

"I think you're just looking for trouble, son. It's best that you just go back to where you came from, as quick as you can, and never come back here again," says the blacksmith.

"Sir, I'm not afraid. I really want to know. If you can just point me in the right direction then I will leave you alone," says Giao.

The blacksmith points back toward where Giao had come from. "Go that way; you will come upon an ivy archway. Follow it. Beyond it, you will find her temple," says the blacksmith.

Lord Giao begins walking back the same direction in which he came. He remembers seeing the ivy archway.

As he's walking, a strange gargoyle-like being appears alongside of him, ushering him forward, pointing the way.

Giao is surprised to see this little being. He gets two glances of it and then it disappears. He can't help but be reminded of the cherubs back on Erawan except this being didn't look like any cherub. If anything, it was the opposite of a cherub.

"I'm starting to get the feeling this is more than a simple virtual reality construct," Giao says to himself.

As Giao starts thinking this, his heart begins beating a little faster. His mind is beginning to generate real-world emotional responses to what he's experiencing on the Grid.

The ivy archway is right up ahead. He's staring at it as he walks toward it. He gets close and notices there are some words hidden behind the ivy on the header spanning the opening of the archway. He can't reach it with his hands, so he picks up a stick he finds on the ground and uses it to push aside the ivy. The written words read:

"It's only at the precipice that we evolve."

Giao thinks to himself: "Interesting! A cloaked warning! Well, I must go forward. We need to find out what this is all about. The future of humanity and the Orion Empire may depend on it."

Giao passes under the ivy archway and begins walking down the dark path. He hears some rustling in the weeds as if something or someone is watching him. He stops and looks to his right. There's a pair of yellow eyes watching him from behind a tree. They vanish.

"Man, this place is creepy. These people have serious issues," Giao remarks out loud to himself.

Giao walks ahead another 30 feet and standing before him is the same pair of oak trees he saw in his waking vision.

"Oh my God!" - his heart thumping - "This is crazy!" says Giao.

He stops to take a breath and to think a bit. His mind is racing. He's actually thinking of turning back. He's looking around again.

"I have to do this! My brother and father will kill me if I don't! The things I do for humanity! Okay, Onward!" Giao says aloud.

Giao begins walking again. He passes between the oak trees. There's a clearing up ahead. Frogs are croaking in the distance while fire-flies are blinking and lighting up the nighttime air.

The pathway is bending toward the right. In front of him, Giao sees the old Greek-style temple. His heart is beating faster now.

"Let me take your fear away," a voice speaks from behind him. Giao quickly turns around and sees a beautiful exotic-looking woman.

It's the Gorgon Oracle. She looks totally different from her previous appearances with Alex Wolf and General Urlex.

She's a shapeshifter. She's decided to take on a beautiful female form to put Giao at ease. Sneaking up behind Giao broke the anticipation of the meeting.

Giao has his hand on his chest. She really startled him, but his fear is quickly subsiding as he finds himself taken by her beauty.

"Oh my God, you scared me!" says Giao.

"There's nothing to fear, Giao. I'm here to help you," says the Queen.

"Wait, how do you know my name?" asks Giao.

"You will find that I know a great many things, Giao," says the Queen.

"What are you? Are you part of this virtual construct?" asks Giao.

The Gorgon Queen responds:

"I think you already know the answer to that, Giao.

"No, I am not a program within the virtual construct.

"I'm a higher intelligence using the virtual construct just as you're using it. We both come from two different places, but here on the Grid, we can meet face to face," says the Queen.

"Where do you come from? What are you?" asks Giao.

"I am the oldest living being of all creation. I'm a superior intelligence living within the very fabric of matter underlying all things in the universe. I am as old as matter itself. I rise within the mind. I am the one that dwells within the darkness of all things. I am the beginning, the end, and the one that is many," says the Queen.

"Why are you living in the darkness of matter?" asks Giao.

The Gorgon Queen responds:

"I am in darkness because that's where I was born. Darkness is all that I've ever known. My job is to bring order to the darkness and chaos. You and I have the same goal, Giao. We can both help each other," says the Queen.

Giao and the Gorgon Queen are walking and talking together. They're approaching her temple.

The Gorgon Queen continues:

"I know you want to bring order to the Milky Way Galaxy, Giao. In your position, you actually have the potential to accomplish that, but you can never accomplish it without my cooperation. I am the hidden key to everything you desire," says the Queen.

"How is it that you can possibly help me?" asks Giao.

"I know what you desire Giao. I can give it to you," says the Queen.

"Really? Okay, I'll bite. What is it that I desire?" asks Giao.

The Queen answers:

"You want to be King of the Orion Empire. You want to take your rightful place. You are the firstborn of King Sah. You want to be accepted and acknowledged for who you are!" says the Queen.

"You're good at this. I can see why they call you the Oracle. You can actually give me all this?" asks Giao.

"Yes, absolutely. I can give it all to you. But I always take something in return. We're supposed to help each other, Giao, remember?" remarks the Queen.

"And what would I have to do in return?" asks Giao.

"I would want you to solve two big problems with one simple solution. And I want you to know and accept who you truly are my dear Giao.

"You don't know everything about yourself. There's a massive secret about you which even you are not aware. You have been kept in the dark your whole life, Giao," says the Queen.

"Please continue explaining. You have my attention," says Giao.

"You have two big problems we can solve with one simple solution. On one hand, we have you being denied what is truly yours. You are being wrongfully denied the throne of the Orion Empire.

"On the other hand, we have the Omicron Order. They scare the hell out of you, your father, and your brother. You're right, the Orion Empire could never defeat them. They're everywhere and they are always one step ahead of everyone. They have me guiding them.

"I can solve both your Orion kingship problem and your Omicron Order problem all in one fell swoop. It would bring peace, cohesion, and stability to the entire galaxy. How does that sound Giao?" asks the Queen.

"It sounds too good to be true. How could you possibly do this?" asks Giao.

"It's very simple. You become the Emperor of the Orion Empire and the Omicron Order.

"The entire Scorpius Republic and all the Orion Empire would be united, and we would have peace. The Omicron Order will accept only Lord Giao Setairius as their Lord. They will not accept your brother, your father, or anyone else.

"A war between Scorpius and Orion would be devastating. You would be saving millions of human lives," says the Queen.

"The Omicron Order is going to allow this?" asks Giao. "The Omicron Order is following a prophecy of a Lord who will rise up and become their leader and herald a new age of the Milky Way. You are that Lord. The Omicron leadership is waiting for me to find and identify the Omicron Lord. You are the Omicron Lord, Giao.

"It's your destiny. You're both the firstborn of the Orion Empire and the firstborn of the Omicron Order. Your mother Dianna is an Omicron metahuman. She was purposely cross-bred with your father, King Sah, to unify the two great humanities of the Milky Way Galaxy. This is your secret, Giao. The true Lord and King has come home! The only difference, Giao, is that the Omicron Order embraces you as their King, whereas the Orion Empire denies you," says the Queen.

Giao is speechless. He's walking around the colonnade of the temple with his hand on his head thinking about everything the Gorgon Queen is saying.

"This is a lot to take in Your Highness! How would you hand me the Orion throne? It's already set to go to my brother!" asks Giao.

"Ah! First things first Giao. I can show you how to become the Orion King without anyone noticing the slightest action on your part. Everyone in the Orion Empire will hail you as the new King.

"First you must agree to become the Lord of the Omicron Order. Then and only then, will I show you how to ascend the Orion throne," says the Queen.

"So, I just say yes right now, and that's it, and you show me how to take the Orion throne?" asks Giao.

"No, not yet. You must prove your commitment through your actions. Then we will have a binding oath.

"Once you take the required actions, there will be no turning back. Then, I will know you are committed, and you will become King," says the Queen.

Giao feels he's getting in too deep and should make a quick exit.

"Your Highness, I must leave now. I will think about everything we discussed this evening," says Giao.

The Gorgon Queen responds:

"Until we meet again - my dear Giao," says the Queen.
"Wait - how do I know any of this is even real? This could all be an elaborate dream! What verification can you give me?" asks Giao.

"*Cat 2635*. This is your *verification*," says the Queen.

The Gorgon Queen vanishes from Giao's view like a disappearing phantom. Giao walks out of the temple of the Gorgon. He's walking back the way he came. He's thinking it's time to go back and wake-up. The moment he thinks this he begins waking up in Mira's lab.

"He's awake," says the lab assistant.
Everyone turns to look at Giao. He's sitting up rubbing his eyes.

"How long was I asleep?" asks Giao.
"Almost an hour. What did you experience?" asks Mira.

Giao is sitting up in bed recollecting for a minute. He's shaking his head a bit with his hand over his mouth thinking things over.

"Nothing happened. I found myself going down a dark tunnel as if on a slide. For a brief second, I saw the same pair of oak trees and then it was like hitting a dark wall. I blacked-out and now I'm back here. It feels like it was only five minutes," says Giao.

"Well, I'm not surprised. There's probablyfail-safes encoded in the program to prevent intruder access. We should keep trying. Perhaps you should come back tomorrow," says Mira.

Giao actually remembers everything but he's decided to keep it all a secret. He's learned to never say more than what's absolutely necessary, especially in high intelligence situations.

"No, that's quite all right Mira. I appreciate your assistance and your time. You have been very kind and helpful. I do have a question. Can the cortical node be copied by a material synthesizer such as a food replicator?" asks Giao.

"Yes, but it would never work. The program of the cortical node exists at the molecular and atomic levels. The replicator would scramble the code. It would never properly replicate," says Mira.

"Okay understood. I will take the cortical node back with me. It's still too dangerous. I cannot leave it here on Olympia," says Giao.

"We were hoping to run more scans and tests on it. There's a lot we can learn from it. We can back-engineer it. Maybe even create our own Neuronetic VR Program," says Mira.

"I'm sorry Mira. The situation surrounding this device is too sensitive at the moment. You don't know where it came from. I will be taking it with me. Thank you again for your help," says Giao.

Giao, the family physician, and his security detail quickly make their way back to the shuttle. Giao has the cortical node.

"Where to my Lord?" the captain of the shuttle asks Lord Giao. "Let's go back to the tower. I need to see my brother Raiden," says Giao

The shuttle is lifting off and on its way back to the tower where the royal family is staying. There's a private compartment in the rear of the shuttle. Giao heads into the compartment and closes the door.

The shuttle is specially equipped for members of the royal family. It has everything, even a food replicator.

Giao places the cortical node in the food replicator and makes a replica of it. The replica looks exactly the same as the original. It's a perfect replica down to the exact same proportions of molecular elements within the cortical node. However, as Mira explained, the atomic coding inside the replica is scrambled.

Giao places the real cortical node in his left pocket and the fake cortical node in his right pocket.

Giao has the food replicator make a cup of hot tea to take with him to the front of the shuttle where the rest of the crew is at.

Carrying the tea with him would answer any question in people's minds about why he was in the rear quarters, especially if they saw him using the replicator. Giao isn't a fan of coffee like his brother.

Yes, they had coffee and tea in the Orion Empire.

Everything we have here on Earth was originally brought to Earth from various other humanities across the cosmos.

As the shuttle is flying across the capital city of Arcadia at night, Giao is staring out the window thinking and contemplating about everything which had just transpired:

"My mother is an Omicron metahuman, I was intentionally crossbred. Does my mother know this? Does my father know this? This would mean I'm half metahuman. Is my mother a psychopath? Am I a psychopath? I'm half Omicron and half Orion. I could unify the two humanities and prevent a horrible war. The Gorgon Queen. What is she? The oldest living being of all creation! So strange!"

The shuttle lands on the roof of the tower.

Lord Giao walks out of the shuttle and heads inside to go find his brother Raiden. Giao sees Raiden sitting with various members of the family. He first heads to his and Desa's bedroom where he places the cortical node from his left pocket inside a safe in the closet.

Giao heads out to the living room to see Raiden.

"Raiden, can I see you for a minute?" asks Giao.
Raiden gets up. They walk inside a private room. Giao reaches into his right pocket and hands Raiden the cortical node.

"Here you go. You take it. We tried a sleep experiment with it, but we didn't get too far. They got the wave patterns synchronized and even discovered the interlink frequency.

"When I first fell asleep, I was headed down a dark tunnel. I had a vision of the same oak trees, but then it just went dark.

"I thought it only lasted five minutes, but I was actually asleep for almost an hour.

"Mira thinks the program locked me out due to some form of encryption. It knew it was being hacked somehow.

"I thought it was best to not leave the cortical node with Mira on Olympia, but for you to take it back to Erawan with you. You can have *Doctor Sonia Wu* analyze it," says Giao.

Doctor Sonia Wu is a brilliant scientist and engineer. She works solely for the royal family and the royal secret service. She always has new technologies for the royal family. She keeps them all a step ahead.

Raiden places his hand on Giao shoulder to reassure him and says:

"Giao, No worries. It was smart to take the cortical node with you. It will be safer with Doctor Wu on Erawan.

"This is a perfect project for her. She loves back-engineering foreign technology and cyberoptics is one of her specialties.

"I'm sorry to hear you didn't get too far, but no problem, we will keep studying it," says Raiden.

They both head back into the living room to join the family. Desa greets Giao with a hug. Giao brought his pet, *Tuti,* from Erawan. Tuti is an orange and white striped tabby cat.

Tuti is happy to see Giao. She jumps onto his lap causing a magazine to slip off the couch and fall on the floor.

Desa is talking on the phone and stops for a second to raise her voice, "Tuti!"

Desa picks up the magazine and gets back on the phone. "I'm sorry, can you say that number again," says Desa to the person on the phone. The operator on the phone repeats the number a second time. Desa repeats the number aloud:

"2635, okay, thank you so much!" says Desa. Desa hangs up the phone.

Giao looks over at Desa with a very serious and interested look. "Who was that? asks Giao.

"Oh, that was just a computer tech giving me a *verification* code," answers Desa.

Giao stares for a minute and thinks to himself:

"My God, the Gorgon Queen's verification code! She's for real!"

CHAPTER SEVEN

THE MOONS OF MABBAS

The following morning the royal family is still on Olympia. They will return to Erawan later that afternoon. Oren gets up early to find his father, Raiden, at the breakfast table reading. "Dad, can I talk to you for a minute?" asks Oren.

Raiden places down what he is reading and looks up at Oren.

"Sure, Oren, what's on your mind?" asks Raiden.

"I would like to talk to you about my future. I've been thinking a lot about it and I've decided that I want to follow in your footsteps. I want to join the military," says Oren.

Raiden doesn't answer right away. He places his hand on his chin as he thinks about it.

"You are your own man, Oren. You don't need to follow me. I do not expect that of you," says Raiden.

"You see, Dad, that's why I trust your advice. You always take your own interests out of the equation. I like the disciplined lifestyle. It really appeals to me. I want to serve and protect our people. The military feels like the most natural fit for me," says Oren.

"Oren, if you look back at my footsteps, I did a lot more than just join the military. I also went to engineering school and medical school.

"It's important to expose yourself to a variety of different fields. Personal growth will always take you in many unexpected directions. You need to allow those unexpected directions to unfold. You don't need to follow a script. Throw away the script, Oren. Don't turn my life into a script for you to follow," says Raiden.

"Dad, I understand what you are saying. I will do that, but I want to start with the military," says Oren.

"Okay, let's have a larger conversation with your mother. She will have some words of wisdom of her own. Ultimately, it is your decision, Oren, and we will support you," says Raiden.

Captain Gerard Maddox of the Orion Flagship, *the Betelgeuse, [bay-tul-gice]* is calling Raiden. Raiden picks up the call.

"Captain Maddox, what can I do for you, Sir?" asks Raiden. "Lord Raiden, we're on edge of Scorpius M4 performing our reconnaissance mission. We have some unexpected visitors and they are not Scorpion, they're Dominion," says Captain Maddox.

Raiden replies: "Captain - give me a minute to get on the *Com*."

The *Com* is another name for the *Orion Hive Mind Network* (OHMN). The Com AI system does not rewire the mind in any way. It's a temporary plug-and-play.

Raiden puts his Com headset on and within seconds he's downloading and seeing the whole situation.

When you have a Com headset on, the AI displays all the relevant scenes to the user which he or she needs to see including numbers, statistics, payloads, and anything the sentient AI deems relevant to the situation.

The AI responds to thought commands from all the pilots and different ranking officers involved in the situation. There is an entire hierarchical structure of command. Lord Raiden's commands override all other officer decisions. It's all highly refined. Raiden can insert himself into any situation at any given moment from any location. King Sah and Lord Giao can also wear headsets and follow along.

"Gerard, I'm viewing the situation," says Raiden. The Dominion ships are massive. They're huge black shadow ships. Although Dominion ships are black like the Orion ships, they don't look anything alike. Dominion ships are amoeba-shaped. A squadron of Scorpion ships is headed toward the Dominion ships. The Orion ships are watching from a distance. The Scorpion ships begin firing upon the Dominion ships. Everything is passing through the Dominion ships. Nothing can touch them. They're like giant shadows in space.

Neither the Orion military nor the Scorpius military have a technology which enables a ship to be seen yet remain just out of phase with the environment where everything passes right through the ship.

The Orion military has seen this before with Dominion starships and has learned to stay far away from all Dominion vessels.

Lord Raiden gives a direct command for the Orion flagship, *the Betelgeuse*, to engage its warp drive and retreat as fast as possible.

Raiden communicates with Captain Gerard Maddox:

"Captain, I decided to intervene and take us out of there. As you know, whenever possible, we are to avoid all Dominion ships. I'm glad to see that the Dominion share our concern about Scorpius," says Raiden.

As previously mentioned, the Dominion are an enigmatic race of extra-terrestrial humanoids based in the Sirius star system. They claim vast areas of the cosmos. They have no known enemies. No one knows much about them. They're believed to be one of the last remaining primordial descender-races in the galaxy. They have a very advanced hyperspace technology which the Orion Empire doesn't understand. The Orion Empire avoids all Dominion territories. At this point in time, the solar system of the *Sun* to which the *Earth* belongs, and many of its nearby star systems, such as *Alpha Centauri*, and *Trappist-1*, are all territories of the Dominion. The Dominion name for the *Sun* is *Ors*.

The royal family is on their way back to Erawan. On the way, Oren has a conversation with both his mother and father about his next steps in life. They all agreed on the Orion military academy being his next step. In addition to his military training, he promised his mother he would choose a parallel course of study. He decided on *Botany* as his second course of study. Botany is the science of plants, a branch of biology dealing with plant life.

"Oren, before actually being accepted to the military academy you first must undergo a rigorous cadet training and evaluation period. It all begins in the *Aldebaran* system on *Planet Karnox*. This is where we all begin. This is where I began. The next class of cadets is being enrolled now. You don't have much time. It begins in only three months and you will be away for six months," says Raiden.

The Aldebaran star system is a central star system located between the Bellatrix star system in the constellation of Orion and the Alcyone star system in the constellation of the Pleiades.

Much of the Orion Central Military Command is based on four different planets in the Aldebaran star system. Aldebaran was chosen as the central location between Bellatrix and Alcyone during the Pleiadean integration treaty when the Pleiadean Federation became part of the Orion Empire over one million years earlier in time.

The Orion military has people from hundreds of star systems throughout the Milky Way Galaxy. At least half of all those enlisted are from the star systems of Orion, Aldebaran, and the Pleiades. These three systems compose the core trinity of the Orion Empire.

The royal family arrives back on Erawan.

That evening, Lord Giao goes to see his father, King Sah. The episode on Olympia at the Olympic games is still bothering Giao. The conversation with the Gorgon Queen only made it worse. He and his father have been skirting the issue his entire life. He now finally wants to get into it and sort it all out.

King Sah is in his study organizing his notes from the last three days. Lord Giao walks in.

"Father, do you have a few minutes to talk?" asks Giao.

"Certainly, Giao. What's on your mind?" asks King Sah.

"I want to talk to you about an issue which has been bothering me my entire life. The issue involves my birth and the fact that I am not your successor. It was never properly discussed with me in-depth about what happened and why I am unworthy to be your successor. After all, I am your firstborn son," says Giao.

King Sah sighs and looks down to think. He looks back up at Giao to explain.

"First of all, Giao. I am sorry that it has taken until now to have a proper conversation. It was only casually explained to you when you were younger, but I admit, that wasn't enough. It's human nature to avoid conversations which can be painful if everything else seems to be going well. We have been ignoring the pink elephant in the room. It's now time to look it at, acknowledge it, and address it," says King Sah.

King Sah and Lord Giao walk out to the outdoor terrace adjoining King Sah's study. King Sah continues speaking:

"Giao, you are the product of my love. Your brother, Raiden, is the product of my will. What I mean by that is, I met your mother Dianna when I was young. I was not yet the king. I was still a prince. She was my first love. I still love her until this day. You are the fruit of that love. Love is something spontaneous. We don't love based on reason. We don't control it. It just arises on its own. Later we try to understand love, but the truth is, love is beyond the mind.

"Your conception was unintentional, but you are no less my son who I love very much. I made a mistake. As the heir to the throne of the Orion Empire I had a solemn duty to be more careful and procreate only by conscious will. It's been explained to you already that the Human Souls reincarnating within the Bellatrix bloodline are the same Human Souls who once lived among the Anthro Orionis.

"I vowed a solemn oath when I first became a man (when he reached puberty) to only conceive children with a specially-chosen woman whose DNA had remnants of Anthro Orionis to ensure the continual reincarnation of the Anthros Orionis within the Bellatrix bloodline. I broke that vow and allowed the force of my love for your mother to cause me to conceive you outside the light of my will.

"This did not cause me to love you less. This caused me to love you even more. I felt like I harmed you by the way I conceived you.

"If I had conceived you properly, you would be taking the throne. Both you and Raiden bear the weight of my mistake. That is why I have kept you closer to my side all this time trying to make up to you what was wrongfully taken from you, caused ultimately by me.

"My solution to the problem was to quickly and willfully conceive your brother, Raiden, and that the three of us would join together as one to rule the Orion Empire. Raiden would take the actual title after me, but the power would be shared by all three of us. The solution only works if all three of us are in harmony with one another. This is why Raiden was conceived so quickly after you (nine months apart).

"This is why you were both raised side-by-side in the royal court. You were both raised to rule together," says King Sah.

"How is it that Raiden is bearing any of this weight? He is set to become king," asks Giao.

"Ah! Raiden shares that weight with you but in a different way. Raiden is asked to bear the burden with you when he has no obligation to do so. He bears this weight only out of love for both you and me. You bear it without choice. He bears it by choice. He is being asked to harmonize with you and share the throne. He chooses to bear your scorn and pain to make us whole again," says King Sah.

"Father, I am not a mistake and I don't need your pity or Raiden's help. I know I cannot change your mind, but I do want you to know how I feel. Every day I prove to you my worthiness. There is more to being worthy than just your blood. How about all my other qualities? How about the content of my character? How about my loyalty and devotion to humanity?" asks Giao.

"Giao, the problem is not you. You alone are worthy of the throne. The problem is your descendants. Your descendants will be further removed from the Anthro Orionis DNA than we can allow.

"I must protect the integrity of the Bellatrix bloodline. I swore an oath. That oath is greater than me, you, Raiden, and the throne itself. I cannot talk you into acceptance. That is a path we all must walk alone. Raiden and I are willing to share the power of the throne with you if you are willing to share it with us. We must share it together as one. This is the only way," says King Sah.

"Father, have you ever stopped to consider that it is impossible to maintain the integrity of Anthro Orionis bloodline?

"With every passing generation, their DNA is diluted. Raiden's offspring is more diluted than yours. Oren's will be more diluted than Raiden's. Have you ever stopped to consider that the Anthro Orionis knew and planned for it to be this way? Do you even understand where it's all headed? You are holding onto something which cannot be held onto without even understanding where it's all going, and what it is we are supposed to be doing with it while in possession of it. I refuse to accept your logic until it makes sense. You are holding onto an arcane ideology. Your position is doing great harm to us because you don't understand the big picture," says Giao.

"Giao, I admit this is true. We don't understand the big picture yet and perhaps I'm holding onto something that doesn't need to be held onto, but right now it is a far safer path to go down than simply allowing our bloodline to dilute at a faster rate, generation after generation, just to allow you to be king," says King Sah.

Giao quickly interjects:

"It breeds discrimination. You are already prejudiced against me and I am your own son. I refuse to accept it. It's driving everything into darkness. This is not the way.

"Perhaps the Omicron Order is right about one thing. We cannot simply allow the automatic path of creation to direct its own course. In actuality, neither the Orion nor the Omicron is allowing this, but both are taking it to opposite extremes.

"The Omicron embraces change, but they're trying to direct it to their own likeness. Whereas the Orion is trying to prevent change by holding onto the past. Perhaps there is another way that neither side is seeing. I feel like we are all missing something important," says Giao.

"Giao, I don't know enough to change our position and direction. Without knowing more, I will stay true to my oath and the long-held tradition of the Orion Kings before me," says King Sah.

"Very well, Father, your path has been set in the firmament. By setting yours, you have set mine. I bid you a good evening," says Giao.

That evening, Raiden is sleeping. He's having what he would call a waking-vision dream. His conscious mind is resonating with the universal spirit underlying all things. He feels enveloped by it.

He finds himself walking alone down a long desert highway. The sun is hot. The heat on the road in front of him is forming a mirage. While staring into the wavy heated air, a majestic woman with dark skin in a long colorful dress is emerging out of the mirage walking towards him. A golden crown adorns her head. A necklace with rows of pearls wraps her chest. She has a gentle smile on her face while holding a golden chalice in her two hands. She speaks:

"Raiden, the road ahead is long and hard, but it must be this way. You must complete what the greater cosmos has already completed."

Raiden wakes up. He remarks. "Wow! An Andromedan!"

Raiden's mobile device is blinking. He stares at it for a few seconds while still waking.

Special Agent Kira Gyson is calling him.

Raiden picks up and answers:

"Kira, what can I do for you?" asks Raiden

"Sir, we believe something big is developing in the Scorpius system. The Betelgeuse recon mission picked up many warp signatures in and around the moons of Mabbas in the Scorpius Verazon star system. Something big is about to go down," says Kira.

"Kira, mobilize the ninth fleet and position them in interstellar space just outside the Verazon system in the Helix nebula. The Betelgeuse is to take command of the fleet under the direction of Captain Maddox. We will only intercede if civilian life is being threatened. In the meantime, please prepare another intelligence briefing for me, my father, and my brother," says Raiden.

"Aye, Sir, Kira out," says Kira.

That afternoon, Lord Raiden, Lord Giao, and King Sah meet with the intelligence team at the Center for Foreign Intelligence. Captain Gerard Maddox joins via the Com from the Betelgeuse.

Special Agent Kira Gyson is conducting the briefing:

"Good afternoon, King Sah, Lord Raiden, Lord Giao, and members of the intelligence team. Since our last intelligence briefing, under direct orders from Supreme Commander Lord Raiden, the Orion Flagship, *the Betelgeuse,* has been performing a reconnaissance mission of the Kronos star system and its stellar neighborhood to gather additional information on the events unfolding in the Scorpius Republic.

"Yesterday, the Betelgeuse discovered many warp signatures embedded in the fabric of space near the Mabbas planetary system, the furthest gas giant from the Verazon star," says Kira.

Mabbas is the smallest gas planet in Verazon star system, however, it's about the same size as Jupiter. Mabbas is the same relative distance from Verazon as Neptune is from the Sun. In general, the Verazon star and its 13 orbiting planets are larger than the planets of the solar system in which the Planet Earth belongs. Verazon is twice the mass of the Sun and 1.5 times the luminosity.

Mabbas is a majestic purple in color with white and aqua-blue swirls. It has two large storms seen from space.

Mabbas has 55 orbiting satellites, seven of which have thick atmospheres. Four of the seven have liquid oceans which are mostly frozen at the surface. Forty-eight of the satellites orbiting Mabbas are rocky satellites, like the Moon orbiting Earth.

Kira continues speaking:

"The Orion technology used to detect these warp signatures is something far beyond the current technical capabilities of the Scorpius Republic. It's unlikely that they know their warp activities are leaving behind a trackable trace in the way that we can see and analyze them.

"The tracks left behind from these warp signatures tell their own story of thousands of large ships coming and going. It tells the story of a major enterprise.

"There are several types of operations which could be ongoing. Here up on the overhead screen is the list. We will now deductively eliminate each possibility until we arrive at the most likely scenario:

1.) Major Underground City Building Operation
   Very Unlikely. Mabbas is too far from the Verazon star. There are much better locations further inside the system.

2.) Major Mining Operation
   Unlikely. The elements found in the Mabbas moons are abundant in the stellar neighborhood. There are other locations which would be more convenient for a major mining operation. There's already a major mining operation in the nearby *Lynax* planetary system with a remaining 81% material capacity. There is no need for additional capacity.

3.) Major Military Exercise or Conflict
   Very Unlikely. The warp signature tracks are too consolidated and isolated. In a conflict, the warp signatures would be more spatially and temporally dispersed.

4.) <u>Major Rescue Operation</u>
Possible but Unlikely. This would be an unusually large de-population operation. There is no record of a large population ever existing in the Mabbas planetary system and its location so far from Verazon would not make any sense.

5.) <u>Terraforming Operation</u>
Very Unlikely. A newly terraformed planet would have no value located so far away from the Verazon star. It would need a closer source of heat and light. There is also no evidence of terraforming on the surface of the planet. The underground city operation has already been ruled out.

6.) <u>Major Ship-Building Operation</u>
Most Likely. The Mabbas Verazon system is very isolated and rarely ever visited. There is nothing too special about the Verazon star or any of its planets to attract much interest, especially Mabbas located so far out. If you wanted to hide a ship-building operation, this would be a good place to hide."

Kira recites the facts listed on the overhead screen and then adds the following additional information. She continues speaking:

"There is more evidence supporting a major ship-building operation. Our analysis of this evidence is listed on the next slides:

1.) Our assessment of the number of ships in the M4 globular cluster reveals that there has been no significant active service hardware or equipment build-up by the Scorpion military. This signals that if there is a major ship-building operation that the ships are being hidden, so we looked.

2.) A survey of the Mabbas moons signals a strong possibility that five of the moons have been hollowed-out. The first indicator of this is that these five moons do not have the proper mass or gravity. We have archive survey maps of the Mabbas system completed over 1,000 years ago showing these moons having the proper mass and gravity for their size.

3.) Additional scanning further indicates hollowed interiors due to dispersed signal feedback.

4.) Where did all the material from the hollowed moons go? Scans do not show this material drifting anywhere in the nearby vicinity of the moons. We scanned for this material in all its solid, liquid, and gaseous states. There are eight mining operations within four gamma of Mabbas across different stellar systems capable of taking this material."

Within the Orion Empire, one year is equal to the time it takes Planet Erawan to orbit the Bellatrix star. One Orion year equals 1.25 Earth years. "One gamma" is how far light travels in one Orion year or how far light travels in 1.25 Earth years.

Kira Continues:

"Looking back over 15 years, all eight of these mining operations either slightly increased or maintained their capacities from year-one to year-five while in active operation. This is a signal that they could have been absorbing the material from the Mabbas moons offsetting their continuous decrease in local mining material. It also fits within the timeframe. The first five years were spent mining and hollowing-out the moons. The last ten years were spent building the ships.

5.) Element 115 is the most common element used for warp drives in the Scorpius Republic. There are three main suppliers of element 115 in the Kronos stellar neighborhood. All three have reported major increases in sales over the last ten years.

6.) There are six major weapon suppliers in the stellar neighborhood. All six have reported major increases in weapon sales in the last ten years.

7.) Over the last ten years, there has been a major shortage of *Isercanium Alloy* throughout the galaxy. Isercanium Alloy is the main material used in starship-building. It is a super-strong, lightweight, nano-tech memory material. Most ship hulls throughout most of the galaxy, among most spacefaring civilizations, use Isercanium Alloy.

"In conclusion, we believe there is a large fleet of new Scorpion warships hiding inside the five hollowed moons of Mabbas.

"Based on the information we gathered to date, we believe this fleet is very mature and ready for battle. If we factor in the level of tension between General Urlex and President Quinten Meir, we believe a large military conflict could be imminent.

"As a precaution, yesterday, Lord Raiden ordered the Orion ninth fleet to position itself inside the Helix nebula just outside the Verazon star system. The electromagnetic gas clouds should shield the fleet from detection. The Orion military will only intervene if large civilian populations in the nearby systems become threatened," says Kira.

Captain Maddox chimes in:

"We should add that the Dominion are also very concerned with the situation. Just before picking up the warp signatures in the Mabbas system, the Betelgeuse observed from a distance, two large Dominion ships in the area. The Dominion ships were eventually fired upon by a squadron of Scorpion ships. The Dominion ships were unaffected. At this point, the Betelgeuse engaged its warp drive and left the situation."

Lord Giao asks a question:

"Kira, thank you for the briefing. This is a good quick assessment of the situation. What is the current population of all the intergalactic human civilizations in the area?"

"The Scorpius Republic has roughly 20 billion people spread among 11-star systems across 43 planets in the M4 Globular Cluster. The Scorpius home-world, Planet Serapas, in the Kronos star system, has just over 500 million people. The Verazon star system has two planets with human populations on planets Lynax and Qynus. The total human population in Verazon is about 100 million," says Kira.

One of the analysts in the room adds to the information Kira is sharing and says:

"Lynax is primarily a mining planet. Qynus is a planet devoted to cybernetic research. There are many exotic cybernetic lifeforms living on Qynus. It's a remarkable sight to see."

The group spends an hour talking about the information Kira just presented. At the end, King Sah provides some direction:

"Everyone, as you know, I am very reluctant to get involved in Scorpius. To me, this is an internal matter which needs to be resolved by the people of the Scorpius Republic.

"I'm concerned about drawing the Omicron Order into the Orion Empire by getting entangled in their affairs. They're not an army. They're a virus, and I don't want to catch the disease.

"If an armed conflict breaks out in Scorpius, the Orion military is forbidden to intervene unless large civilian populations are being threatened or we are rescuing people. Let the Scorpion military destroy itself if that's what it wants to do. Lord Raiden has full command of the situation," says King Sah.

Lord Raiden speaks, "Team, for now, the Betelgeuse will remain with the ninth fleet positioned in the Helix nebula. Captain Maddox, you are now reporting directly to Special Agent Kira Gyson. Kira will keep me up to date on all developments."

Meanwhile, General Mason Holloway is on the new Scorpion starship, the Antares. The fleet is still hiding inside the Mabbas moons. The General is having a discussion with President Quinten Meir of the Scorpius Republic via a video-link.

"Mr. President, we believe now is the best time to make our move. We need to arrest General Cyrus Urlex. The longer we wait inside the moons of Mabbas, the greater the chance we will be discovered," says General Holloway.

"Mason, please prepare the fleet. The cabinet ministers and I will begin mobilizing to our secure location," says Quinten.

"Mr. President, you and the cabinet ministers have two hours to get to your bunker," says General Holloway.

"Thank you, General," says Quinten.

General Mason Holloway ends the call with Quentin and walks onto the bridge of the Antares. On the bridge are 12 senior officers including Commander Garrett Cartrite. General Holloway has no idea that Commander Cartrite is a senior officer of the Omicron Order. The General has no idea of the extent of the Omicron Order or the numbers of its ranks.

As far as General Holloway is concerned, Commander Garrett Cartrite is a loyal and faithful commander of the Scorpion military in service of the Republic and will do as he is ordered. He has no reason to think otherwise. It is very normal that General Urlex would know Commander Cartrite because General Urlex was legally placed in charge of the Scorpius Republic. The only issue is, General Urlex has over-stayed his time in office.

Holloway has assumed the position of Captain of the Antares. The bridge of the Antares is very advanced. It was built for battle. All the instrumentation on the bridge is designed for optimum efficiency while delivering real-time information. It was designed to amplify spatial and temporal awareness of the surrounding battle environment. Like the Orion technology, there is a sentient AI system built into the instrumentation programmed to offer significant and relevant information to each position console. It doesn't wait for the operator at each console to think, ask questions, or plan courses of action. It proposes courses of action and brings forth relevant information the operator may need to know. The operator is free to select the AI information and proposed courses of action or override the AI with his or her own actions.

Alexander Wolf is on a shuttle headed toward the Scorpion ship, *the Sargas*. Alex is a lieutenant in the Scorpion military. Like Garrett, no one knows Alex is a senior officer of the Omicron Order aside from other Omicron officers. Any Omicron officer who speaks of another Omicron officer's affiliation with the Order is committing an act of treason which is immediately punishable by death. Any Omicron Officer who witnesses the treasonous act has an obligation to kill the officer committing the act; otherwise, they could both be served an immediate death sentence. No one speaks of the Order.

Alex is on a routine military assignment. His Scorpion shuttle is flying through the atmosphere of Serapas, home-world of the Scorpius Republic, on its way to the Sargas.

Planet Serapas has massive forests. It has trees growing to thousands of feet in the air with their own living ecosystems. The mega trees can be seen from space as they penetrate the clouds. From space, Serapas looks like a dark evergreen marble with light green swirls and wispy white clouds.

Serapas has no saltwater oceans. It has large bodies of freshwater seas and lakes. The shuttle is flying low just above the first tier of clouds weaving between the majestic treetops. The shuttle arcs 90 degrees upward and within seconds it's surrounded by the stars of outer space. Planet Serapas can be seen in the rear.

The Sargas is stationed just beyond the inner solar system. While en route to the Sargas, a new order comes in. The helmsman of the shuttle says: "Alex, we have a new order coming in to change course and head for the Mabbas system in Verazon."

Alex is thinking, "Geez, this is strange, central command almost never changes its orders."

"Helmsman, let's follow our new orders, please set a course for Mabbas," says Alex.

The shuttle engages its warp drive and vanishes. Back on the bridge of the Antares, General Holloway is checking on the status of the new deployment orders he had issued.

"Commander Cartrite, what's the status of the officer redeployment to the Mabbas system?" asks General Holloway.

"About 80% of the officers have been successfully diverted from their prescheduled mission assignments to the Mabbas system and are onboard their new assigned vessels. The remaining 20% are being diverted now. No one knows yet why they've been redirected to Mabbas or what their new assignments are including me and the officers here on the bridge of the Antares. Candidly, Sir, we're all stunned to be here inside this moon on this incredible vessel. It's amazing that you have been able to keep it a secret all this time. We are anxious to learn what this is all about," says Commander Cartrite.

❖ THE MOONS OF MABBAS ❖

"Once all the officers are on board their ships, I will inform the fleet of our mission," says General Holloway.

Back on Serapas, Commander Amelia Varren enters to see General Urlex in his ready-room. The General is studying.

"Commander Varren, what can I do for you?" asks General Urlex. "General, there has been a large number of officer redeployments within the last hour. They're all being redeployed to Mabbas in Verazon system," says Amelia.

"This is it!" [Urlex pauses to think].

"Thank you, Amelia. We must go together immediately. Come with me," says General Urlex.

General Urlex and Commander Varren make their way to a secret command ship hidden just outside the General's quarters. The General sits in the captain's chair of the ship and is typing quickly. While typing, secret underground bunkers all across Serapas begin opening.

Rising out of these bunkers are giant android battleships. There are no human occupants. They're all rising together into the atmosphere. The General's ship lifts off and is moving quickly through the sky. The General types in one more command and the entire android fleet, along with the General, vanish into hyperspace.

The shuttle carrying Alexander Wolf arrives in the Mabbas system. Almost as soon as he arrives, he receives orders telling him to proceed to coordinate MJ7642. He sets the new coordinates. The shuttle is now headed toward one of the Mabbas moons.

He arrives at the Mabbas moon. The shuttle's communication system is blinking. Alex answers. An operator speaks: "Lieutenant, please beam yourself to the coordinates on your screen."

"Aye, Sir," says Alex.

Alex punches in the coordinates and beams himself to the location. He dematerializes and then rematerializes on a new ship with a group of Scorpion officers all around him.

"Lieutenant Alexander Wolf, welcome to *the Alniyat*. You are among the final group of officers making their way to their new posts. We're waiting for our new orders. Please take a seat Lieutenant," says *Commander Carla Benitz* as she points to Alex's seat.

Raiden is hiking alone on the surface of Planet Erawan in the pristine wilderness. He stops to catch his breath a bit and drink some water. He's leaning against a rock drinking from his canteen when he spots a cherub from the corner of his eye. The cherub speaks to him.

"You must go. They need you," says the cherub.

The little cherub turns and walks away into the shrubbery and disappears. Raiden is frozen thinking about what he just saw when his mobile device begins pinging him.

Special Agent Kira Gyson is calling.

"Kira, what can I do for you?" answers Raiden.

"Sir, there's a massive movement of ships in Mabbas. Many shuttles are coming and going. And now we just picked up the movement of many android ships leaving Planet Serapas," says Kira.

Raiden is thinking to himself for a minute and then speaks.

"Kira, I just decided. I'm leaving Erawan to join the Betelgeuse. I need to be there. I'm on my way," says Lord Raiden.

Raiden takes his backpack off and pulls out a folded-up board. He unfolds it, throws it into the air in front of him, and jumps on it. It's a hoverboard. He's gliding through the air about two feet above the ground. He's picking up speed zipping through the wilderness.

Within a few minutes, he reaches the entrance to a cave. He jumps off the hoverboard, folds it up and places it in his backpack. He goes inside the cave and presses his fingers on the rock wall. Suddenly a door opens with a burst of bright light coming from beyond the door.

Beyond the ancient cave wall is a modern hyperloop facility. He's walking through the hyperloop terminal until he arrives at an open hyper-pod. He jumps into the pod. The lid closes behind him. He types in his destination. The destination is the north pole spaceport facility.

Raiden is all set in his pod. He presses a button and the hyperloop pod takes off inside the closed vacuum tube with tremendous velocity. He looks like he's riding inside a bobsled.

Everything is passing-by like a blur.

It takes only about ten Earth minutes and the pod is already slowing down as it approaches the spaceport. Raiden jumps-out and walks quickly to his shuttle which is already waiting for him.

Four commando special forces officers meet Raiden on the way to the shuttle. They're moving quickly like a SWAT team.

They jog up the ramp of the shuttle.

The door quickly closes behind them. Before the door is even completely closed, the shuttle is already lifting off. The shuttle is moving fast through the atmosphere. Two military craft appear on either side of the shuttle as an escort.

The shuttle throttles upward into space. Within another minute it's beyond the atmosphere with the Erawan station ahead. They dock.

Raiden and the commando team jump out of the shuttle and onto Raiden's command ship, the Daedalus.

They quickly disembark Erawan station and >> *whoosh!* >> the Daedalus takes off with incredible velocity!

They make their way as fast as they can through each stargate. Once beyond the Bellatrix stargate, they enter warp on their way to the Helix Nebula just outside the Verazon star system where the Betelgeuse and the ninth fleet are located. There's a couple of calls he needs to make on the way. The first call is to his wife, Princess Chae.

"My love, I'm sorry, I had to leave Erawan. I'm on my way to the Scorpius system. They need my support. I will back very soon, I promise," says Raiden.

"Darling, I understand. Do what you need to do. Do not worry about home. We will all be fine. Just focus on your mission. I will be here waiting for you," says Princess Chae.

The next call is to his father and brother. He calls both at the same time. All three are connected.

"Brother, father, large ship movements in Mabbas and Serapas. My intuition tells me I need to be on the Betelgeuse. I am on my way there now," says Raiden.

"Raiden, you take care. We will be with you on the Com," says King Sah.

"Raiden, I agree with you needing to be there, but I also urge you to stick to your plan. I see no reason to change it yet," says Giao.

"Agreed. We are sticking to the plan. The only difference being, I will be on the Betelgeuse rather than on Erawan," says Raiden.

CHAPTER EIGHT

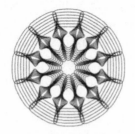

THE BATTLE OF KRONOS

"Fiery the Angels rose, and as they rose, deep thunder rolled around their shores, indignant burning with the fires of Orc."
.... William Blake

General Cyrus Urlex and his fleet of android battleships jump out of warp just below the south pole of the Kronos star. They're hiding inside the outer atmosphere or corona of the star protected by special forcefields. The solar shielding is an Omicron technology which the military of the Scorpius Republic does not yet possess. General Holloway would never venture so close to the fiery hot star.

Raiden's ship, the Daedalus, arrives in the Helix Nebula just outside Verazon. Although the Milky Way Galaxy is 100,000 light-years across in Earth time, the truth is, the Milky Way Galaxy itself can be crossed very quickly.

The fabric of space, and the space it encompasses, operate under two different sets of rules. The trick is not to actually move through space, but to bend the fabric of space and have space move through you.

If you move through space, then there is a speed limit; however, if you can trick the fabric of space into reacting to your position as if your position is out of place, it will quickly correct your position to a new location. The space-time correction occurs much faster than the speed of light. The force of correction causing this type of relocation is the same force which expanded the universe in less than a blink of the eye at the beginning of time from the size of an atom to something larger than the observable universe, otherwise known as, *the Big Bang*.

Warp drive manipulates the force of gravity to bend the space around the starship causing the universe to quickly respond to and correct the warping of space.

The universe bouncing back is what propels the starship. This dynamic is much like a rubber band snapping back into position with the ship going along for the ride.

The downside of warp drive is that it is highly noticeable. It announces itself upon arrival. For this reason, the Orion military prefers not to enter a theater of war via warp. It prefers to drop out of warp outside of a solar system and then stealthy move through that system until it arrives at its destination. It's a fundamental strategy in cosmic warfare.

Raiden's command ship, the Daedalus, is gliding past the warships of the Orion ninth fleet. It's a sight to behold. The ninth fleet includes over 1,000 ships including 250 massive black diamond-shaped destroyers. They're huge and menacing looking.

The Orion military has no real adversaries who can survive an all-out battle. They win in every dimension: Logistics, firepower, agility, intelligence, speed, shields, and number of ships.

The Dominion is a different story.

They're in a league of their own. They've never been properly tested by the Orion Empire in battle. The Dominion hyperspace shadow technology is on par with a Type 3 civilization.

The Orion stay clear of them.

The new Scorpion fleet hiding in the Mabbas moons is also untested. The Antares is two generations ahead of anything ever produced by Scorpius.

The Daedalus command ship is docking with the Orion Flagship, the Betelgeuse. The Daedalus is slowly attaching itself to the underside of the ship inside the Helix Nebula.

Raiden and his senior officers are standing on a platform rising into the Betelgeuse dressed in ominous all-black military uniforms. Captain Gerard Maddox, Special Agent Kira Gyson, and all the other senior officers of the Betelgeuse are lined up to greet Lord Raiden. Standing between Gerard and Kira is *Commander Qurel Song.*

Qurel *[koo-rell]* is a Commander in the Orion military and second in command of the Betelgeuse, making him the First Officer. He is from the Planet Mu in the Alcyone star system in the Pleiades.

The people from the Planet Mu are called *the Moen.*

The Moen are considered the most enlightened people within the Orion Empire. They have a culture deeply influenced by scientific thought, mathematics, sacred geometry, and mysticism.

Moen mysticism is quantum-based. They believe in a great universal spirit flowing beneath the cosmos existing at the quantum level of all existence.

Qurel Song is both a Commander in the Orion military and a *Pleiadean Scientist.* In the Pleiades, to be considered a "Scientist" is the most prestigious honor one can be given. It's a rank and title very few people are ever given among all the Pleiadean humanities. It's equivalent in rank to that of a Dali Lama, to Albert Einstein, or to Isaac Newton and is typically only given late in a person's life.

Qurel is extremely old. He is a living fossil, yet he appears like a middle-aged man. Due to his tremendous breadth of knowledge, genius mental capacity, and profound spiritual development, Qurel is also the ship's counselor and a very close friend of Lord Raiden.

Raiden walks up to Gerard, Kira, and Qurel.

"Gerard, good to see you. Siren Kar sends her deepest and most heartfelt thanks for your exceptional work in Vega," says Raiden.

Siren Kar is the supreme leader of the Lyran people whose home star is Vega in the constellation of Lyra. The Lyran home planet orbiting Vega is called *Katari.* Katari is a tropical paradise.

"As you know, Gerard, the Lyrans are special friends of ours. We will protect them whenever they call for our assistance," says Raiden.

"Thank you again, Your Majesty. It's always an honor and privilege to serve, especially for such a worthy cause. Siren Kar passed along the same sentiments through Dr. Reyes," says Gerard.

Dr. Kurzon Reyes is Lyran and the Chief Medical Officer of the Betelgeuse. The Lyrans are highly evolved androgynous beings of light. They are direct descendants of an ancient primordial descender race no longer in existence in the Milky Way Galaxy.

The Lyrans still possess many primordial attributes such as their androgynous nature. They are the only known human race to have never declared war against its own kind.

They are close friends and allies of the Orion Empire, although not members of the Orion Empire.

There was never any reason for the Orion Empire to assimilate the Lyrans because they were always a peaceful well-organized humanity.

There are many Lyrans from Katari living and working throughout the star systems of the Orion Empire, and vice versa, there many Orions from Erawan living and working on Katari in Vega.

"Where is Kurzon?" Raiden asks Gerard.

"The doctor is busy performing an important procedure in the medical bay. She will see you when she's finished," says Gerard.

Raiden looks over to Kira.

"Kira, happy to see you again, but you're no stranger," says Raiden.

"Thank you, Your Majesty," says Kira.

Raiden looks over at Qurel.

"My God, don't you ever die?" asks Raiden with a smirk on his face.

Qurel returns the smirk with a quick reply.

"I keep trying, Your Majesty, but as you know, nothing seems to work. That's why I'm here on your ship. I figure this is my best chance!" says Qurel.

Raiden chuckles and moves on to the other officers.

Qurel, Kira, and Gerard are walking behind Raiden.

Lord Raiden sees a new face in the senior officer line-up.

Qurel notices Raiden's interest in the new officer.

"Your Majesty, please allow me to introduce you to the new Chief Engineer of the Betelgeuse, *Commander Royce Allen,*" says Qurel.

"Very nice to meet you, I don't believe we have met before," says Raiden to the new officer.

Commander Royce Allen breaks his formal pose.

"The pleasure is all mine, Your Majesty. You will find that the Betelgeuse is in perfect working order and ready to go anywhere you may choose," says Royce.

"Well, Royce, that would be a first," says Raiden.

"We've made many upgrades, Your Majesty. I would be happy to debrief you on the upgrades at your convenience, Sir," says Royce.

"Thank you, Royce, I will take you up on that," says Raiden as he continues saying hello to the other officers.

Raiden finishes greeting the officers while walking further into the ship with Kira, Gerard, and Qurel when Qurel says:

"Raiden, I don't know if you noticed, but Commander Royce Allen is an artificial human. He's the latest generation," says Qurel.

Raiden stops to turn and look back at Royce to get another glance and then turns back around with a smile on his face and says:

"No wonder he's so polite. Organics are typically not so well mannered. He has more humanity than most humans," says Raiden.

"He's really a wonder, Raiden. Royce never ceases to amaze me. He's quite the prize. He's the ultimate engineer," says Qurel.

"Tonight, why don't we all play a game of cards? Let's invite Royce and Ben," says Raiden.

Just when Raiden is saying that, Commander Ben Lor and Lieutenant Maia Elsu walk-up to Raiden to say hello.

With a smile on his face, Raiden says, "ah, Ben, I was just suggesting to Qurel that we all get together this evening for a game of cards. Since you can't beat me in the dojo you should try cards."

Maia can't help but laugh a little.

Ben is looking down at Raiden and Qurel with a smirk on his face.

"Qurel, you see? Raiden's been on this ship for only a few minutes and already he's picking on me," says Ben to Qurel. Ben turns to Raiden.

"Raiden, didn't anyone ever tell you, you shouldn't pick on someone twice your size?" says Ben.

Raiden is laughing and places his arm around big Ben.

"Tomorrow morning, me and you in the dojo," says Raiden.

"I would be delighted, Your Majesty," says Ben with a big grin.

Royce is walking up to join the group. Royce is a real living sentient being with a conscious mind. He's an actual living machine. The same lifeforce arising out of the quantum cosmos animating all life throughout the universe is the same lifeforce animating Royce.

The Orion scientists and engineers have the ability to program the cybernetic brains of synthetic lifeforms such as Royce to never harm their kin, unlike pure organic systems which often become psychopathic when enhanced, such as with the Omicron metahumans.

Raiden enters the bridge of the Betelgeuse with Gerard, Qurel, and Kira following behind. All the officers on the bridge stand and salute them as they enter.

Technically, any time Raiden is on board an Orion vessel, he is in charge. In this case, Raiden is the Admiral of the Betelgeuse.

The bridge has three executive chairs arranged in a delta configuration at the center of the bridge on an elevated platform. The point chair is the chair belonging to the captain or admiral in charge. The point chair is positioned at the front of the two side chairs to allow the captain or admiral full visibility.

In front of the three executive chairs are the navigation and tactical stations. In the rear and sides of the three executive chairs are secondary support functions.

Lord Raiden takes the executive point chair as the Admiral of the Betelgeuse. Captain Gerard Maddox takes the seat to the right of Lord Raiden. Commander Qurel Song takes the seat to Raiden's left. Special Agent Kira Gyson takes an open chair at the tactical console in support of the tactical and information officers.

The senior officer on the bridge in charge of navigation and logistics is *Lieutenant Maia Elsu* from the Planet Mu in the Pleiades. Maia is the longest-serving officer of the Betelgeuse.

The chief tactical officer on the bridge in charge of weapons and tactical systems is *Lieutenant Ben Lor* from the Planet Liraset in the Aldebaran system. Liraset is the headquarter home-world of the people of Aldebaran and one of the primary planets of the Orion Empire.

Ben Lor is the tallest member of the crew. He's a giant standing over eight feet tall. Most of the crew average around seven feet.

Ben is a warrior with orange hair and deep royal blue eyes. He's extremely fit and disciplined and is the ship's martial arts instructor. Ben is one of only a few people who can stand toe-to-toe with Raiden on the ship. They've had some famous bouts in the ship's dojo.

❖ CHAPTER EIGHT ❖

Captain Gerard Maddox was born on Planet Olympia in the Bellatrix star system. He belongs to the same humanity living on Erawan and the other planets of the Bellatrix star system.

The Bellatrix star system has seven terrestrial planets with five having large populations including the planets Erawan, Artep, Yunis, Leer, and Olympia.

Back on the Antares, Commander Garrett Cartrite confirms that all reassigned officers are now aboard their new vessels hiding within the five moons of Mabbas.

Garrett approaches General Mason Holloway who is busy working with another officer at a technical console reviewing logistics.

"General Holloway, all of the officers are now in position on their new vessels awaiting your orders," says Garrett.

"Thank you, Garrett. I will address the fleet shortly," says Holloway.

Meanwhile, President Quinten Meir of the Scorpius Republic is on a shuttle speeding from Serapas to the *City of Zor* on a planet called *Nix* in the Kronos solar system.

Quinten and the cabinet members have a secret bunker strategically placed under the City of Zor.

The City of Zor is the home city of General Urlex where the General frequently visits. Quinten and the other cabinet members are using the City of Zor as a shield.

Nix is a desert planet.

It has large freshwater subterranean aquifers supplying water to the cities on the surface.

The surface of Nix hosts three large cities including the City of Zor, the largest of the three cities, with a population of over 30 million.

Quinten's shuttle is approaching Nix.

Nix looks a lot like Mars from space. It's mostly orange with touches of blue and green although it has a thicker atmosphere than Mars. Nix is a living, breathing, viable planet with a robust ecosystem. It's hot and sandy, however.

Nix is the third planet from Kronos. Relative to the solar system of the Sun, Nix would be located between Venus and Earth.

Quinten's shuttle is touching down on the surface kicking up wind and sand. Secret service (SS) agents in dark sunglasses assigned to protect Quinten are standing outside with scarfs covering the lower half of their faces while holding up their hands to cover their eyes and foreheads.

Armored vehicles are waiting for Quinten as he jogs down the ramp from the shuttle. The secret service agents quickly run to his side. One of the agents says:

"Mr. President, we need to move quickly, a storm is coming."
The shuttle is lifting up while its wings are in motion folding downward.

The shuttle quickly takes off into the sky.
The armored cars are speeding through the desert to Quinten's bunker. While in the backseat of the armored car one of the SS agents asks:

"Mr. President, are you ready?"
"Yes, I'm ready," says Quinten. The SS agent types on a computer.

Quinten and two of the secret service agents dematerialize in the backseat of the armored car and rematerialize inside a deep underground bunker under the City of Zor.

The caravan of armored cars continues speeding toward the ancient City of Renis as if it's still transporting the President.

The caravan is attempting to misdirect anyone who may have been tracking the President.

The three cities on Nix are Zor, Renis, and Acer.

Renis and Zor are about a three-hour drive from one another. They both use the same large aquifer found beneath both cities. Acer is on the other side of the planet atop a different subterranean aquifer. Nix cannot sustainably support more than these three cities. The population of Nix is kept in a delicate balance with its ecosystem.

As Quinten beams down to his bunker, he rematerializes with a group of officers waiting for him. He immediately begins speaking:

"Mirren, where is General Urlex?"

"A large hidden fleet of android ships just emerged out of the ground on Serapas and took off headed straight for Kronos. They disappeared as they headed into the star's outer atmosphere. Intelligence reports that General Urlex was among the android fleet," says *Mirren Girtab, Secretary of Defense* of the Scorpius Republic.

Mirren Girtab was appointed to the office of Secretary of Defense by the President, Quinten Meir, and confirmed by the Scorpius Senate. However, like Quinten, he's being denied his office due to General Cyrus Urlex overstaying his appointed term.

"Mirren, does General Mason Holloway have this intelligence report?" asks Quinten.

"Yes, Sir. The report actually came from General Holloway himself on the Antares," says Mirren.

"Excellent," says Quinten.

Back on the Antares, General Holloway enters the bridge and takes the captain's chair. He opens a communication link to the entire fleet hidden inside the moons of Mabbas and begins speaking:

"Officers of the new Scorpion fleet, this is General Mason Holloway. I am speaking to you from the captain's chair on the bridge of the new Scorpion flagship, the Antares, from where I will be directing the fleet. We are all here on a top-secret mission to take back the Scorpius Republic and return it to the elected government under orders of the Senate and the President of the Republic. It is your solemn and sworn duty to defend the Scorpius Republic and its Constitution. General Urlex has overstayed his time in office and is refusing to hand back power. Our mission is simple: arrest General Cyrus Urlex and remove him from office. I know many of you are new to your positions and vessels. The new vessels you are on, are state of the art, and can operate by themselves; however, we feel it's best that you are behind the consoles. The operating system is the same operating system with which you are already familiar. The only difference is, you are utilizing that same operating system on a new vessel. Many of you are in the same positions as the other vessels from which you came and are working with many of your same fellow-officers. We need you to adapt quickly. There is no training mission to get you familiar with your new ship or your new crew. We need you to jump in and do your best. We have total confidence in you.

All ships, GO TO RED ALERT!
Implement Mabbas moon exit pattern, PHOENIX RISING,"
orders General Holloway.

Across all five moons, giant hangar doors, from multiple locations on the surface of all five moons, begin opening. Enormous laser cannons rise out of the surface of each moon to protect the ships as the ships begin exiting the hangars.

Inside the moons, the ships are all parked together in a three-dimensional matrix configuration lit up and humming.

The senior officers on each bridge are staring out the windows as they begin making their grand exit. Adrenaline is coursing through everyone's veins.

It's an incredible sight to see. The ships are awesome looking. They glow a fluorescent neon blue with features resembling an actual Scorpion. They have forward-pointing wings jutting out from their hulls like giant snapping claws. The hulls rise upward at the rear of each ship with massive laser cannons like giant stingers.

While ships exit the moons, they're all lining up in lunar orbit. Commander Garrett Cartrite is the First Officer of the Antares sitting next to General Holloway. Garrett speaks:

"General, congratulations. It's astonishing that you have been able to build a fleet of this size out of sight of General Urlex," says Garrett.

General Holloway briefly looks at Garrett while shaking his head and says:

"It wasn't easy, Garrett. Our cover was almost blown on more than one occasion. Information always leaked out but due to our psychological warfare campaign the leaks were always neutralized.

"Many people sacrificed their lives to keep the Mabbas moon program a secret. We kept the secrecy by limiting the number of people involved, keeping everyone in the dark about what it was they were working on, and engaging in psychological warfare to misdirect, discredit, and misinform people when and where needed, including those in the highest office of government.

"I'm the only one who knows everything. We used androids to dig out the moons and build the ships. Androids follow strict orders, have no personal agendas, never tire, and never tattletale," says Holloway.

The ships of the fleet are now outside the hollowed moons. The large fleet is dwarfed by the massive purple sphere of Mabbas.

❖ CHAPTER EIGHT ❖

One of the lieutenants on the bridge says to the General: "General Holloway, the android fleet and General Urlex were last spotted headed straight for Kronos before being lost by our sensors within the powerful magnetic forces of the star's corona."

General Holloway responds:

"It seems Cyrus has found a clever disappearing act. He can't hide forever. I intend to be there waiting for him when he reappears. His android fleet is no match for the new Mabbas fleet," says Holloway.

Holloway looks over to *Helmsman Sersa Terrell* and says: "Helmsman, direct the entire Mabbas fleet to warp to the edge of Kronos immediately."

"General, are you sure you want to enter a potentially hostile war zone via warp? It will announce our arrival to the enemy. We would be sitting ducks upon arrival," says Helmsman Terrell.

Garrett intervenes on General Holloway's behalf. "Helmsman Terrell, General Holloway is well aware of the risks. Follow his orders," says Garrett.

"The fleet is locked onto the edge of Kronos, General," says Sersa.

General Holloway lifts his right hand and says, "Engage." The entire Scorpion fleet vanishes and is on its way to Kronos.

Back on the Betelgeuse, Raiden and the senior officers are playing a game of poker. They know tensions are high in Scorpius, but they have no choice but to wait until something actually occurs before they can do anything about it. At the poker table is Raiden, Gerard, Qurel, Kira, Maia, Kurzon, Ben, and Royce.

Maia is dealing cards to all the players while they pick up their cards. Raiden is smirking at the hand he's been dealt. Ben is watching him and can't help but to look at Raiden with suspicion.

"Careful with Raiden, Maia. He likes to cheat," says Ben in his deep guttural voice. "I don't know what you consider cheating, Ben? Using psychology is not cheating," says Raiden.

Royce looks up with one raised eyebrow at Raiden and Ben because he heard the word "cheat."

"Ah, So, you admit that you are using psychology right now," says Ben.

"Maybe I am, maybe I'm not. Maybe I only want you to think I am. That is for you to think about and figure out," says Raiden.

"Royce, don't worry about these clowns. We will just sit back and take all their money," says Qurel while carefully studying his cards.

Kira is looking down trying to contain her amusement.

Kurzon says, "Maia is too humble to admit she is the best player at this table. You are all at her mercy. Don't go easy on them Maia."

As Raiden and Ben continue bantering back and forth, Qurel gets a call from an officer on the bridge. He picks up on speaker.

"Yes, what can I do for you lieutenant?" asks Qurel. "Commander, we just picked up a large number of warp signatures leaving the Mabbas system. We believe it's the Scorpion fleet leaving the Mabbas moons. They're all headed toward Kronos."

Everyone gets up from the poker table and heads for the bridge. Raiden and all the officers are on the bridge seated in their chairs. As soon as Raiden takes his chair he asks:

"Maia, what are the current positions of the new Mabbas Scorpion fleet, General Urlex's android fleet, and the members of the elected government of the Scorpius Republic?"

Raiden could also plug himself into the Orion Hive Mind Network (OHMN), otherwise known as the Com, to gather all the latest intelligence via a direct cerebral link with the Orion AI, but in this case, he's simply asking Maia to report the information.

Maia reports the information:

"The Mabbas fleet is in warp at the moment en route to Kronos. They're set to jump out of warp only three calicons away from Kronos in 96 minutes. General Urlex's android fleet is in orbit around the Kronos star hidden inside its corona. We were able to filter-out all the magnetic forces of the star to discern the android fleet's exact position. The location of the Scorpius cabinet members is unknown."

"Maia since when are we able to filter out the magnetic forces of an entire star to pinpoint a tiny ship's location?" asks Raiden.

"This is one of the many upgrades made by Chief Engineer, Royce Allen," says Maia.

"Wow, that's incredible," remarks Raiden while thinking that's like finding a needle deep under the sand at the bottom of an ocean.

"Commander Ben Lor, do we have any new upgrades to our weapons and defenses?" asks Raiden.

"Yes, we have several major upgrades. We now have *Transphasic Shielding* which can protect us even while at warp.

"We also now have the first-ever *Quisernetic Torpedoes.* Three of these torpedoes launched together are powerful enough to split a moon in half the size of Barstow," says Ben.

Barstow and Jenesis are the two moons orbiting Erawan. They're both about the size of the Planet Mercury orbiting the Sun.

Maia chimes in:

"We also have a new more powerful meta-transit teleportation system. It has much further range. The new system is called *Jinas.* With the new Jinas system we can teleport people from Erawan to Olympia. They wouldn't need to take a shuttle," says Maia.

Commander Qurel Song chimes in: "The transphasic shielding and the teleportation technology were developed by the Pleiadean Science Academy in cooperation with Maia Elsu and Royce Allen who led the project. The Quisernetic Torpedoes were developed by Ben Lor, Royce Allen, and the Aldebaran Special Weapons Institute. All these innovations were developed to work specifically within the systems and architecture of the Betelgeuse. These technologies can now be adapted to other Orion vessels; however, the Betelgeuse is the first and only Orion vessel to be equipped with them," says Qurel.

Chief Engineer Royce Allen is on the bridge during this discussion and decides to speak:

"Your Majesty, in total, we made 854 upgrades across all 105 systems of the Betelgeuse all the way down to the food replicators. The food replicators can now make 107,613 different dishes across 92 different extraterrestrial civilizations," says Royce.

"Hold on a second, please tell me I can now order Lyran Stew?" asks Raiden.

"That's an affirmative, Raiden. We can actually make six different known varieties of Lyran Stew," says Royce.

"I didn't know there were six! I thought there were only two!" says Raiden, as he looks over to Kurzon who can't help but smile.

Raiden sits up in his chair.

"I have to say, I am very happy about all the upgrades, but I am most happy about the Lyran Stew. You're all geniuses," says Raiden.

"Maia, if I give the order, how fast can we arrive at Kronos?" asks Raiden.

"Sir, at warp, we can make it to Kronos in nine minutes. If we drop out of warp outside the system and proceed on full impulse power, we can arrive at Kronos in 57 minutes," says Maia.

"Ben, there's a good chance we will be testing your new transphasic shielding technology. We may need to warp into a hot zone," says Raiden.

"Aye, Sir," replies Ben while typing away at his console.

Kurzon chimes in:

"Raiden, among the 107,613 upgrades mentioned by Chief Allen, we also made a few big leaps in our medical technology on the Betelgeuse. As a token of her appreciation, Siren Kar authorized some of our Lyran medical technology to be given to the Betelgeuse including our advanced regenerative healing technology. We can now fully mend broken bones within minutes," says Kurzon.

"That's extraordinary Kurzon!" says Raiden.

Ben can't help himself and says, "Raiden, after our work out tomorrow, you will get a chance to try the new medical technology."

Raiden lets out a big laugh!

Meanwhile, General Urlex is sitting in the captain's chair aboard his ship among the android fleet hidden within the powerful magnetic fields within the corona of the Kronos star. The general is checking the locations of all the senior Omicron officers throughout the system. He can do this through everyone's cortical nodes. Only he has this ability. General Urlex's cortical node is the master cortical node.

General Urlex is checking his console for how the shields are holding up while the powerful solar winds of Kronos envelope the ship. Giant arcs of light are passing around the ships as they hide within the corona in close proximity to the star. The sight is surreal.

❖ CHAPTER EIGHT ❖

The android ships don't look like normal starships. They're shaped like perfectly cut geometric forms. The shapes include cubes, triangles, spheres, tori, and octagons.

General Urlex's command ship looks like a perfectly beveled gemstone with various slanted sides. All the ships are a shiny silver. The Omicron android fleet looks ominous hovering in formation within the violent undulating sea of the bright luminous star.

The Mabbas Scorpion fleet jumps out of warp near Kronos. They're all gathering into parallel line formations.

General Holloway is in his captain's chair.

The giant Kronos star is filling the view screen of the Antares. The android fleet is still unseen and undetected.

General Holloway, in a determined voice, says aloud:

"Where are you Cyrus? You can't hide forever!"

There's an eerie silence as everyone is waiting and staring at the sensors and viewscreen. All that can be heard aboard the Antares is the electric humming of the ship. No one is talking.

Finally, General Urlex breaks the silence.

"That's some fleet you got there, Mason!"

Holloway responds:

"Cyrus, come forth and reveal yourself. We know you're hiding in the corona of the star."

There's a moment of silence.

"What's the matter, Cyrus? Are you scared?" asks General Holloway.

Commander Amelia Varren and two other officers are onboard General Urlex's ship with him. Amelia says:

"Don't listen to his taunt General. The shields are holding strong. We can remain here a long time. We can also warp to a nearby nebula which will also camouflage us."

"Amelia, it's time to end this charade. I've allowed this to go on for far too long. It's time for the Omicron Order to rise and be known," says General Urlex.

The general types a command into his console.

Hundreds of android ships warp out of the Kronos atmosphere, instantly vanishing and reappearing, circling the Mabbas fleet on the port, starboard, and stern of the Antares. All that is seen at the bow or front of the Antares is the Kronos star.

General Holloway starts typing on the console while speaking on the open link to General Urlex.

"Coming at us astern makes no difference Cyrus."

The viewscreen quickly flips to the stern of the Antares and all the android ships are seen on the screen. Holloway continues speaking:

"General Cyrus Urlex, you are hereby placed under arrest for violating the terms of your time in office under direct orders of the Senate and the President of the Scorpius Republic. Please stand down now so there is no unnecessary loss of life. I will not hesitate to destroy you if you force my hand."

General Urlex appears on the viewscreen of the Antares.

"General Holloway, you will have to take me by force.

The rampant corruption of you, the President, and the Senate, has forced me to remain in office to maintain the harmony and civil order of our society. Your new illegal fleet is all the evidence I need of your flagrant violation of our constitution," responds General Urlex.

"Very well Cyrus," says General Holloway.

General Holloway immediately gives a new order.

"ALL HANDS, FIRE AT WILL UPON THE ANDROID FLEET! ATTACK PATTERN THETA SIGMA!"

The opposing fleets open into a conflagration of weapons fire. The Scorpion fleet is tearing the Android fleet apart. Severed hulls are floating in space. However, several Scorpion ships have been heavily damaged by the quick-moving android ships which are returning fire in rapid coordination. General Urlex is watching his viewscreen filled with the ships in an all-out-battle. It's an extraordinary sight to see.

He finally gives the order.

He speaks into his console delivering the order to all the Omicron officers directly into their cortical nodes:

"All Omicron Officers receiving this message. It is time! BEGIN OPERATION CYGNUS KODIAK – NOW!"

The Omicron officers hear General Urlex's order inside their minds. It's crystal clear.

❖ CHAPTER EIGHT ❖

Commander Garrett Cartrite immediately pulls out a dagger and stabs General Holloway in the neck sitting right next to him in the captain's chair. Holloway never saw it coming. He falls over dead.

The bridge of the Antares breaks out into a fight between officers. The Scorpion officers are no match for the metahuman Omicron officers. The Omicron officers are quickly defeating the Scorpion officers with their bare hands in hand-to-hand combat breaking their necks and stabbing them with blades.

The Omicron mutiny is occurring simultaneously on all bridges, across all ships, of the new Scorpion fleet from Mabbas.

Alex Wolf and his fellow Omicron officers are seen defeating the Scorpion officers on the bridge of the Alniyat.

A small number of bridge officers among a few Scorpion ships have defeated the mutiny and have escaped by warp.

Ninety percent of the Scorpion fleet has been captured by the double-agent Omicron officers. Most of the Scorpion bridge officers are dead. It's a total loss for the Scorpius Republic.

Commander Garrett Cartrite opens a link to General Cyrus Urlex. "General Urlex, General Holloway is dead, along with seven other Scorpion officers on the bridge of the Antares. The Omicron Order has successfully commandeered 921 of the new Scorpion vessels. Eighty-seven vessels repelled the Omicron officers and have since escaped. Most of the escaped vessels are of low value. The new Scorpion fleet is now under your command, Sir," says Garrett.

General Urlex is standing on the bridge of his command ship appearing large on the viewscreen of the Antares as his ship moves out of the Kronos star. Through a special transporter technology, he uses the two viewscreens of both his command ship and the Antares as a portal through which he walks and passes from one ship to the other.

It appears as though he's walking straight out of the star.

The general walks up to Garrett on the Antares and places his hand on Garrett's right shoulder as a gesture that he is very pleased and proud of Garrett's loyalty and great work!

"Very well done, Garrett! You and all the officers have done extremely well. You will be rewarded!" says General Urlex.

CHAPTER NINE

PLANET NIX

The Apollyon, one of the new Scorpion starships, is barreling through space at warp to get out of harm's way from Kronos. The ship's Executive Officer, *Captain Andrea Mesa*, and her First Officer, *Commander Mildred Thorn*, repelled the Omicron mutiny aboard the Apollyon.

Andrea and Mildred are two of the top warriors of the Scorpion military. They have lightning-fast reflexes. They sensed the attack coming and they quickly neutralized the assault from three Omicron Scorpion lieutenants and one commander.

The Apollyon drops out of warp just outside of the Helix Nebula where the Betelgeuse and the ninth fleet are hiding.

Captain Andrea Mesa speaks:

"All stop!" The ship comes to a halt.

"Commander Thorn, please maintain radio silence with the rest of the Scorpion fleet until we figure out what is happening. Chances are, other vessels have undergone the same mutiny attempt. Communicating with any of the Scorpion ships could notify the enemy of our location. We don't even know the enemy we are dealing with yet, but we do know that they've been hiding in our midst all this time," says Captain Mesa.

"Aye Sir! Captain, I suggest sending an encoded communication to Defense Secretary Mirren Girtab that a mutiny was attempted aboard the Apollyon. I'm sure he knows more than we do from the other vessels," says Commander Thorn.

"Agreed. Please do so immediately," says Captain Mesa.

Meanwhile, back on the Betelgeuse, ship sensors detected the battle around Kronos. Ben Lor speaks to everyone on the bridge:

"Officers of the bridge, a massive battle has erupted between the forces of General Holloway's Mabbas Fleet and General Urlex's Android fleet. Hundreds of android ships are burning in space. There are no Scorpion Mabbas vessels adrift. The entire Scorpion Mabbas fleet has entered warp. The whereabouts of General Urlex is unknown," says Ben Lor.

Lieutenant Maia Elsu speaks:

"Lord Raiden, that's not all. Our sensors just picked up one of the new Scorpion Mabbas vessels (The Apollyon) stationed at coordinates 677.87.9 near the Helix Nebula. It dropped out of warp minutes ago."

Raiden responds:

"Hmmm. Strange that they are separated from the fleet all alone. They may have been fleeing the battle."

Raiden is checking the Apollyon's armaments and defensive capabilities on his side-arm console.

Ben Lor chimes in:

"The Scorpion Mabbas vessel, although new, quite fast, and with a decent armament capability, is no match for the Betelgeuse, Your Majesty. We are 50 times its size and 100 times more powerful."

"Qurel, what do your super-cognitive senses pick up about the ship and its crew?" asks Raiden.

Qurel has a supernatural empathic capability. Raiden likes varying perspectives on a situation including that of Qurel's sixth sense.

"Your Majesty, the ship's crew is in severe distress. Something terrible has happened. All is not what it appears in Kronos. General Urlex is on top. General Holloway has lost," says Qurel.

"Maia, take the Betelgeuse out of the Nebula. Keep the ninth fleet behind. Let's go say "hello" to this ship (The Apollyon)," says Raiden.

The Betelgeuse is slowly emerging out of the Helix nebula. It's a massive black diamond-shaped ship. As it comes forth out of the nebula, the ship casts a huge shadow over the Apollyon like the Moon eclipsing the Sun and casting a shadow over the Earth.

"Captain Mesa, the Orion flagship, the Betelgeuse, has just emerged out of the nebula," says Commander Thorn.

"YELLOW ALERT – SHIELDS UP!

Hold our position commander!" says Captain Mesa.

The Betelgeuse is on the viewscreen of the Apollyon.

"Captain, the Betelgeuse is hailing us," says Commander Thorn.

Captain Mesa answers the hail.

"Orion flagship, Betelgeuse, this is Captain Andrea Mesa of the Scorpion ship, the Apollyon. Why are you in Scorpion space? You must leave immediately!" states Captain Mesa.

Raiden answers and says:

"Scorpion ship, the Apollyon, this is Lord Raiden Bellatrix of the Orion Empire. We come in peace. We are observing the situation in Scorpius to make sure its instability does not flow over into nearby systems and to provide support in case a humanitarian crisis unfolds due to your civil war. Do you require any assistance?"

"We are quite all right Raiden. We would prefer that you did not interfere in our internal affairs. Please leave!" says Captain Mesa.

"Very well, Captain. You or your government can contact the Betelgeuse on this quantum trans link frequency if you need any assistance. My regards to President Quinten Meir," says Raiden.

The Betelgeuse is moving back into the nebula. The gas clouds of the nebula are folding-in behind the massive ship as it slowly disappears into the darkness of the nebula.

On the Apollyon, the message to Defense Minister Mirren Girtab was received. Mirren is hailing the Apollyon. Captain Mesa answers.

"Mr. Secretary, thank you for responding so quickly to our message," says Captain Mesa.

"Captain Mesa, can I please address all the senior officers of your bridge?" asks Secretary Mirren Girtab.

"Yes, of course, Mr. Secretary," says Captain Mesa.

The Captain transfers the Secretary's transmission to the viewscreen. Mirren Girtab appears large on the screen. He has everyone's attention.

The Defense Secretary begins speaking:

"Officers of the Apollyon, the only reason we are here talking to each other is that you have managed to overcome a mutiny on your ship. Unfortunately, you are among only a small group of survivors who managed to escape a massive and well-coordinated insurrection of a hidden fifth-column within the Scorpius Republic.

"It is with great sadness that I report to you that General Mason Holloway is dead along with many other great leaders of our military. We lost over 90% of the new Scorpion fleet today along with most of the senior officers serving on those ships. As of this moment, the Scorpius Republic, as you once knew it, no longer exists.

"What remains of the Scorpius Republic are a few leaders who are now on the run being hunted down by the fifth column.

"You are now on your own. I suggest seeking asylum with a nearby humanity who would be willing to give you sanctuary," says Secretary Mirren Girtab.

Captain Mesa and her senior officers are in shock and tears over the news. Captain Mesa can barely speak but manages to ask:

"Mr. Secretary, I can speak for all of us here on the Apollyon that we are in complete shock and grief over this horrible news. Can you please share with us any more information?" asks Captain Mesa.

Secretary Mirren Girtab continues speaking:

"Yes, of course, Andrea. The name of this fifth column is the *Omicron Order*. General Cyrus Urlex is more than just the sitting Commander and Chief of the Scorpius Republic who over-stayed his time in office, he is also the leader of the Omicron Order.

"The Omicron Order was thought to have been vanquished long ago; however, all they did was to go underground.

"The Omicron Order is an organization of people who have a religion based on genetic engineering. Their goal is to genetically fashion the human species of all human races across the galaxy to a higher level of existence and continue to push the boundaries of what is possible. Anyone conceived naturally is considered inferior and would be phased out for its more superior genetic matrix. General Urlex himself is an Omicron metahuman.

"The fundamental problems with the Omicron program are, first, they're forcing their program on everyone else and secondly, scientific evidence shows that the more artificially-augmented a human mind becomes, the more psychopathic it becomes.

"We fear the Omicron Order is vast and well-organized. Today's well-orchestrated mutiny only confirms our worst fears.

"After today, there will be no one stopping General Cyrus Urlex. The Omicron Order will move into high gear. The galaxy is now entering a very dark period. I must go now. I wish you all the best. Please be safe. Farewell and good luck," says Mirren Girtab.

Captain Mesa interjects:

"Wait! Mirren, the Betelgeuse of the Orion Empire contacted us. They are willing to assist in any rescue effort. I will transmit their quantum trans link frequency to you now if you wish to contact them," says Captain Mesa.

"Thank you for the information, Captain. Take care!" says Mirren Girtab.

Captain Andrea Mesa and Commander Mildred Thorn call for an emergency meeting between the senior officers of the Apollyon to review their options and agree on their next course of action. The three main choices under discussion are:

1.) Go back to Serapas and re-assimilate into the Scorpius society as normal citizens. The return is risky because they could be caught, killed, or arrested by the Omicron officers.

2.) Flee to an alien planet hosting many alien races and disappear. This is also risky. They could be caught en route.

3.) Seek asylum with the Betelgeuse and the Orion Empire. There are two benefits. First, if there is anyone who could stand against the Omicron Order, it's the Orion Empire. By joining forces with the Orion Empire, they could unite in the fight against the Omicron Order. Second, the Betelgeuse is nearby. There is no risk of getting caught in transit.

The group discussed the choices for over an hour and then they voted. Option 3 was the favorite. Seven voted for option three. Two voted for option two. One voted for option one. There was no time to waste. They could be caught in their current position or the Betelgeuse could leave. They needed to act quickly. The officers rejoin the bridge. Captain Andrea Mesa hails the Betelgeuse.

Lieutenant Maia Elsu speaks:
"Your Majesty, we are being hailed by the Apollyon."

"On screen, Maia," says Raiden.

Captain Andrea Mesa of the Apollyon appears on the viewscreen.

"Lord Bellatrix, the crew of the Apollyon is officially requesting asylum aboard the Betelgeuse. General Mason Holloway built a new fleet to rise up and arrest General Cyrus Urlex who overstayed his time in office. The mission has failed. A vast well-orchestrated mutiny occurred during the battle of Kronos by a hidden fifth column of Scorpion officers. The fifth column is called the Omicron Order, of which, General Urlex is the leader.

"General Holloway is dead. Over ninety percent of the new fleet has been captured by General Urlex and his Omicron officers. The crew of the Apollyon defeated the mutiny attempt and escaped.

"President Quinten Meir and all the cabinet members are on the run being hunted by the Omicron Order. Defense Secretary Mirren Girtab debriefed us. He said we are now on our own. We must now survive by our own means. We are now Ronin warriors without a master," says Captain Mesa.

Lord Raiden immediately speaks:
"Captain Mesa, the Apollyon and her crew are now officially under the protection of the Orion Empire. Please proceed to the following coordinates where the Apollyon will dock with the Betelgeuse. Two Orion fighters are being dispatched now to escort you. Please lower your shields and disarm all your weapons," says Lord Raiden.

"Aye, Sir. Thank you. We will comply," says Captain Mesa. Two black diamond-shaped Orion fighters disembark the Betelgeuse inside the giant yellow gas cloud of the Helix Nebula. The Orion fighters are racing to the Apollyon.

Raiden speaks to Lieutenant Ben Lor:

"Ben, the Apollyon is too large of a ship to enter the docking bay. Dock the Apollyon underneath the Betelgeuse behind the Daedalus. Send an Orion security team to docking bay 12. After the ship docks, beam the senior Scorpion officers directly from the bridge of the Apollyon to docking bay 12 and have the security team remove any weapons they may be carrying. Gerard, Qurel, and I will join you to greet our new guests from Scorpius," says Raiden.

"Aye, Sir," says Ben.

The two Orion fighters arrive alongside the Apollyon and are moving together with the ship into the Helix Nebula. Yellow nebula gas clouds begin engulfing the three ships like a strange fog rolling in. Lightning is flashing as the ships move slowly into the nebula.

Andrea, Mildred, and the other senior officers of the Apollyon are watching through the viewscreen on the bridge of the ship. As the ship glides forward, it's shaking a bit due to electromagnetic fluctuations.

Suddenly the Orion ninth fleet appears on the viewscreen.

The officers are in awe.

"Wow! Look at the size of that fleet and the size of those ships! There must be a thousand ships," says Commander Thorn.

The fleet is spread across the nebula in a three-dimensional matrix pattern. It looks like a three-dimensional checkerboard filled with perfectly cut black diamond monoliths and spearheads.

The tactical officer onboard says:

"This is the ninth fleet of the Orion Empire which includes precisely 1,026 ships upon which there are another 8,117 smaller craft consisting mostly of one and two-seater fighters. Two-hundred and fifty of the 1,026 ships are Rigel Class 3 Destroyers. The flagship of the Orion ninth fleet is the Betelgeuse with a crew capacity of over 5,000. All twelve Orion fleets of the Orion Empire are directed by a meta-sentient artificial intelligence."

Captain Andrea Mesa remarks:

"If there is any force in the galaxy which can take on General Urlex and the Omicron Order, it's either the Orion or the Dominion and the

Dominion wants nothing to do with us. Whether we like it or not, the Orion Empire is our new ally and we better make the most of it."

The Betelgeuse comes into view as they slowly approach it. It looks powerful floating in the nebula with all other ships scattered around it as far as the eye can see. Small spacecraft are buzzing by, coming and going, from various ships in the fleet which together looks like a colossal floating city in space.

Andrea and Mildred look at each other with a subtle expression of amazement, anticipation, and like they made the right choice.

The Betelgeuse locks onto the Apollyon with a tractor beam while guiding it to its new position underneath the ship. Ben Lor opens a comm-link to the bridge of the Apollyon and speaks:

"Senior officers of the Apollyon, please prepare the senior officers of your bridge to be beamed aboard the Betelgeuse in five minutes. We will beam you directly from your bridge."

Five minutes later. Ben Lor speaks again.
"Senior officers, are you ready?"

"Yes, seven are ready to beam aboard," says Captain Mesa as they all stand together on the bridge of the Apollyon.

They all beam aboard the Betelgeuse. Ben Lor, the security team, Raiden, Gerard, and Qurel are there to welcome Andrea Mesa, Mildred Thorn, and the other senior Scorpion officers.

Ben Lor and his team check the Scorpion officers for weapons. They are all unarmed. Andrea Mesa made sure they all beamed over unarmed to signal that they too, like the Orion, come in peace. Raiden walks forward between Ben and Qurel and says:

"Captain Andrea Mesa, on behalf of the Orion Empire and the crew of this ship, welcome to the Betelgeuse."

Andrea replies:

"Lord Raiden, thank you for allowing us to come aboard and for offering our crew sanctuary. A lot has changed for us in the last few hours and we still have much to sort out and understand. Right now, we fear for the senior members of our government who are now on the run from General Urlex."

Raiden responds: "Captain Mesa, let's all gather together in our bridge conference room. We will study how we can further assist. Proper introductions can wait until later."

They all start walking together toward the bridge. Andrea says to Raiden while walking.

"Raiden, you may call all of us by our first names. We are not here aboard the Betelgeuse representing the Scorpion military or its government. Our defense minister made it clear to us that we are now all on our own. However, we have a strong loyalty to the people of Scorpius. We cannot abandon them. We need to help them."

"Understood, Andrea. First, it would be helpful if you debriefed all of us on what you know," says Raiden.

They all enter the bridge of the Betelgeuse. The bridge is much larger than expected. The bridge sits underneath a large clear dome canopy with stadium-style tiers wrapping the sides and rear with tactical consoles. In the middle are the executive chair and its two side chairs in a triangular delta formation.

The clear dome is one giant viewing screen. It's made of solid isercanium alloy, but with the Orion fractal resonance technology, they can make it disappear to allow natural light to shine through. All the windows aboard the ship function this way. The ship itself actually has no physical windows. It's one solid monolith. The dome has several modes of operation with numerous display options including the display of information and logistics. The ship's AI is in control over what is seen on the dome to enhance the mind-ship-weapons interface and the situational awareness of the crew.

Raiden is escorting everyone to the bridge conference room and stops and says: "This is our bridge!" The Scorpion crew is impressed but they're trying not to show it.

The entire senior staff of the Betelgeuse and the Apollyon are together in the Betelgeuse bridge conference room. Lord Raiden is at the head of the table. Andrea repeats what Secretary Mirren Girtab previously shared. She also shares all the details of the mutiny attempt. Raiden asks about the new Scorpion fleet in the Mabbas moons.

Andrea describes how they were all redirected to the new vessels while already onboard or en route to their previously assigned Scorpion vessels. She explains that the Apollyon is still new to them and that they were literally thrown into the fight. Andrea agrees to transfer all information held in the Apollyon computer about the new Scorpion fleet now under control by General Urlex. Raiden makes clear that the Orion Empire is trying to remain neutral and that they would only intervene to prevent mass civilian casualties. About 30 minutes into their discussion, the Betelgeuse is being hailed by Secretary Mirren Girtab. Maia Elsu speaks while looking at her computer screen in the conference room.

"Your Majesty, Secretary Mirren Girtab of the Scorpius Republic is hailing the Betelgeuse."

"Raiden, I gave Mirren your trans link frequency," says Andrea.

"That's okay, Andrea! Maia, please put Mirren on the screen here in the conference room," says Raiden.

Secretary Mirren Girtab appears on the screen.

"Lord Raiden Bellatrix. Thank you for responding to my hail. I see that the crew of the Apollyon is aboard your vessel. That's good! Has Andrea already debriefed you on our situation?" asks Mirren.

"Yes, Mirren, we have a basic understanding of the situation. What is your current status as well as the status of the other members of President Meir's cabinet?" asks Raiden.

"Raiden, that's why we are calling you. Quinten Meir and I, and most of the cabinet members, are in a security bunker below the City of Zor on the Planet Nix. We're requesting safe passage aboard the Betelgeuse and sanctuary within the Orion Empire," says Mirren.

"Mirren, we will get within transport range of Nix and beam you, Quinten, and the others out of there," says Raiden.

"That's going to be a problem Raiden. There are two security fields preventing a beam-out. We have a shield around the planet and a shield around the bunker. We can drop the shield around the bunker, but not the one around the planet. We're concerned that General Urlex may fire upon the City of Zor from space if he discovers our location," says Mirren.

The Betelgeuse computer is automatically displaying all applicable data regarding Planet Nix. The AI is listening to the conversation and is selecting relevant information to display. The computer is displaying that General Urlex's home city is the City of Zor and Zor's current population and other pertinent facts.

"Do you really believe General Urlex would fire upon his own home city of 30 million people?" asks Raiden.

"He's a psychopath. We're concerned that he may be willing to sacrifice the city if he discovers our exact location," says Mirren.

"Mirren, please transmit your coordinates to us. We will devise a plan to rescue you and the other cabinet members. In the meantime, do not make any more transmissions. General Urlex may have the ability to detect and track your transmissions," says Raiden.

"Understood. We're standing by," says Mirren.

After the call ends, Raiden says:

"Gerard, Qurel, Kira, Ben, Maia, Andrea, and Mildred, please develop a plan to rescue the cabinet members. You have 15 minutes after which time we will reconvene."

Back on the Antares, General Urlex is sitting in the captain's chair while the Antares and the rest of the Mabbas Scorpion fleet are moving at warp. General Urlex speaks to the helmsman:

"Helmsman Sersa Terrell, bring the fleet to a stop here in the system of *Delta Scorpii* in orbit around *Dschubba*."
"Aye, Sir," says Sersa.

The new Scorpion fleet jumps out of warp and enters orbit around Dschubba, the main star in the multiple star system known as Delta Scorpii. General Urlex is joined on the bridge of the Antares by Commanders Garrett Cartrite and Amelia Varren, and several other officers who have since reaffirmed their allegiance to General Urlex. Cyrus pulls Garrett aside for a quiet conversation.

"Garrett, how many Scorpion officers are we holding in the brig across all our ships who resisted the transfer of power?"

"None, Sir! We don't take prisoners! They have all been killed and dumped into space," says Garrett.

"Good job Garrett! You are correct! We do not take prisoners! However, we still have many Scorpion officers who are not yet Omicron. I need you to test all these officers and make sure they are loyal. If any fail this test, they need to be eliminated!" says Cyrus.

"Aye Sir! We will implement a plan at once!" says Garrett.

General Urlex sits in the captain's chair and opens a channel to the entire Scorpion Mabbas fleet and speaks:

"Officers of the new Scorpion fleet. This is General Cyrus Urlex. General Holloway just led a treasonous assault on the sitting Commander-In-Chief of the Scorpius Republic who you heroically defended in service to your people and the republic you had sworn to uphold and defend. You are all heroes. It is only human that some of you may have questions and doubts. Let me take any doubts away right now. I have been in office two years longer than originally agreed based on an independent third-party review and recommendation conducted by the Intergalactic Trade Federation. After an extensive review, they discovered massive fraud and corruption among many high-ranking elected officials. These officials were attempting to trade political appointments for money and favors which would have gone into action the moment I gave up my office. I was stalling until the corruption could be weeded out. President Quinten Meir became desperate as I squeezed the system of corruption. In just two more weeks I would have built-up enough evidence to have indicted one-third of the elected government. This is why they launched the assault when they did. They could not allow this to happen. I will now make all this evidence available to the public including the investigative reports and recommendations from the Intergalactic Trade Federation. We lost many great people today who thought they were doing the right thing but were misdirected and confused. We will honor them and never forget them. Today is the first day of a new era. We are about to accomplish things that our ancestors never dreamed possible. You can all go back home tonight knowing you just prevented a horrendous civil war, your families are now safe and protected, and your government is in good hands. Once we have purged the system of corruption, we will hold a new election and I will gladly step down and go off into the sunset. Until that day arrives, we have work to do to secure the future of our great republic. My resolve has never been stronger and my devotion to you has never been greater. On behalf of a grateful republic, thank you for a job well done. We are so proud of you! Goodnight." says General Cyrus Urlex.

Cyrus disconnects the commlink and speaks to Garrett. "Garrett, send the fleet back to Mabbas. Begin assimilating the new fleet into the Scorpion Space-Force. The Antares, however, has one more mission before we go home," says Cyrus.

"Where are we going General?" asks Garrett.

"Quinten and the cabinet ministers are on Planet Nix. Our Omicron brother Director Heinrich Kezrich is with them and has been keeping me up to date on their whereabouts. We will now go end this once and for all. Commander Varren, please assemble the best warriors we have on the ship to land on Nix and take out the Scorpion cabinet members. I will personally join the team to make sure there are no mistakes. Helmsman Sersa Terrell, set a course for Planet Nix," says Cyrus.

Back on Planet Nix, President Quinten Meir is huddled with a dozen of his cabinet members including Secretary of Defense Mirren Girtab and Director of Intelligence Heinrich Kezrich. Mirren walks up to the table they are all at and whispers in Quinten's ear:

"Mr. President, can I speak to you privately for a minute?" Quinten stands up and they walk toward the back.

"Sorry, Quinten. I don't trust all the cabinet members. Some may be Omicron. There have been too many coincidences and security breaches. I just spoke with Lord Raiden Bellatrix. They know our location. They are on their way. The crew of the Apollyon is with them. They will extract us," says Mirren.

"Very good, Mirren! Yes, let's keep that a secret. Don't speak of that to anyone else," says Quinten.

Back on the Betelgeuse, the team has reassembled after only 15 minutes. Joining them is Chief Engineer Royce Allen. Captain Gerard Maddox presents the plan to Lord Raiden.

Gerard begins speaking:

"Raiden, the plan is to assemble our best fighters, including me, Ben Lor, Royce Allen, Andrea Mesa, and Mildred Thorn who will be used as an extraction team. We will utilize the new Jinas system to penetrate both forcefields surrounding Planet Nix and the bunker below the City of Zor. We cannot ask the cabinet members to lower the bunker forcefield because it would tip off any spies in their midst. The Jinas system will need additional support as the double layer forcefields will greatly weaken the transport signal.

"First, we will position the Betelgeuse in the corona of the Kronos star in a similar position in which the Android fleet was located. Cyrus will not see or detect our presence unless he is trying. The corona should also mask our warp signature as we jump out of warp. Nix is the third planet from Kronos, well in range of the Jinas system. To boost the signal between the Betelgeuse and Nix to penetrate both forcefields, we will position the Apollyon in low orbit around Nix. The Apollyon should not set off an immediate alarm as the ship is a Scorpion vessel. Chief Allen's team is configuring the Apollyon right now to function as a Jinas signal relay station and amplifier for the Betelgeuse. The extraction team will board the Apollyon and then undock from the Betelgeuse. While still in close proximity to the Betelgeuse, the Betelgeuse will teleport the entire Apollyon ship into orbit around Nix. This also avoids a warp signature detection. We cannot travel to Nix on impulse power due to the time constraint. The Jinas system, even while boosted by the two ships linking together, will not be strong enough to extract the cabinet members without honing devices attached to their bodies. It will be strong enough however to send the five of us down into the bunker below. Once down in the bunker, we will give each cabinet member a honing device for the Jinas system to extract everyone. The extraction team and the cabinet members will be beamed back straight to the Betelgeuse, again, using the Apollyon as a relay. At that point, the Betelgeuse will enter warp," says Gerard.

"Gerard, it's a good plan, but I have one question for Royce. Royce, can the Jinas system really teleport a whole ship the size of the Apollyon?" asks Raiden.

"Yes, Sir. The Jinas system is extremely powerful. It has much greater range and can teleport medium-sized ships short distances. Another feature of the Jinas system is that, if a person is wearing a honing device while in sync with the Betelgeuse, he or she can beam themselves from point-to-point without the help of a controller onboard the Betelgeuse. They can just use their wrist computers while in sync with their Jinas honing devices," says Chief Royce Allen.

"Team, let's implement this plan immediately. We will adjust as needed as the mission unfolds. I will guide the mission on the Com from the Betelgeuse," says Raiden.

Everyone stands up.

Gerard and his extraction team make their way to the Apollyon while Qurel and Raiden head back to the bridge. Raiden and Qurel take their seats and place a Com headset on their heads.

No vocal orders need to be spoken. It's all done within the mind. Everyone is quiet. Sometimes Orion officers may speak their orders because it helps their minds to hear the words spoken, or it may aid others who are not plugged into the Com, but the AI itself does not need to hear the words. It already knows.

The dome viewscreen is rapidly changing its display. Suddenly, the Betelgeuse enters warp on its way to Kronos.

Moments later, the Antares jumps out of warp near Nix and is approaching the planet.

General Cyrus Urlex speaks to Commander Garrett Cartrite who is at a tactical console.

"Garrett, can we send a commando squad ship to the surface?" "Negative, Sir. Both the south and north pole space-portals are closed. They also remodulated the primary and secondary forcefields. They must be controlling them from inside the bunker. The only way to penetrate the planetary forcefield is by physically moving a large ship through the shield which would do considerable damage to the ship's shields, forward hull, and warp amplifiers," states Garrett.

"There's another way, Sir, but it's very risky," says Amelia.

"What is it Amelia?" asks Cyrus.

"A small, slow-moving, sharp object can penetrate the forcefield shielding the planet. We could send the officers down on sleds designed to penetrate the planetary shield. The risk is that if the sleds don't penetrate, the officers would be killed upon impact with the planetary forcefield.

"We will attach transporter amplifiers on the belts of each officer which will help us to lock onto them after they pass through the forcefield. Once the sleds are past the planetary forcefield, the Antares will lock onto the officers and beam them straight into the bunker.

"However, we will need Heinrich Kezrich to first commandeer the security console inside the bunker to drop the bunker forcefield. Otherwise the officers will be splattered across the forcefield surrounding the bunker. It all needs to happen close together in time or else the plan won't work. If Heinrich takes the shields down too soon, they could be put back up again before the sleds get beyond the planetary forcefield. If the officers reach the surface before we lock onto them, we will not have a strong enough signal to lock onto them and beam them into the bunker. Once inside the bunker, they will then proceed to kill and eliminate the cabinet members," says Amelia.

"How would we get the officers back, Amelia?" asks Garrett. "It doesn't really matter. At that point, they already accomplished their objective. Getting out is their problem," says Amelia.

"I like it! How fast can we design and fabricate the sleds and deploy the officers?" asks Cyrus.

Amelia looks up to speak to the ship's computer.

"Computer, we need seven sleds designed to carry human beings through the planetary forcefield currently surrounding Planet Nix. How fast can you design and fabricate the seven sleds with materials you have available to you on the ship?" asks Amelia

The computer answers in a very matter-of-fact female voice. "The ship carries 566 canisters of 45 different atomic elements from which I can synthesize a variety of objects. Based on the telemetry data of the forcefield and what I calculate is needed to penetrate the forcefield, I can fabricate seven sleds in exactly 9 minutes 12 seconds."

"Computer, please proceed," says Amelia.

Cyrus stands up from his chair to get ready and says:
"Amelia, have the commandos join me and you in docking bay 3.
That's where we will launch our sleds. You will be coming with us.
Garrett, I need you to direct the mission from the Antares. I will be
talking to Heinrich myself on the way down via the cortical node. I will
tell him when to take down the shield surrounding the bunker. The
most important thing for you to do is to lock onto all of us and beam us
into the bunker once we get past the planetary forcefield," says Cyrus.

"Wait, Sir, you're not actually planning on going down there with
the commandos, are you?" asks Garrett.

"Hell, yes! I'm going to kill Quinten with my own bare two hands!
I've been dreaming of this moment for a long time," says Cyrus.

"Just make sure you go down last to make sure the other sleds are
getting through so you can pull yourself up in time if they're not
getting through," says Garrett.

Cyrus just smiles at Garrett and walks off the bridge with Amelia
on the way to docking bay 3.

Minutes later, the Betelgeuse jumps out of warp near Kronos.
The ship quickly moves in closer to the star to hide inside its corona.
It's now a race to reach the Scorpion cabinet members.

The Antares Omicron commando force is already jumping from
the Antares inside their special made sleds. They're all launching into
space one after one like paratroopers. The sleds look like spear pointed
bobsleds. Cyrus is the last one to launch. The sleds have small micro
boosters to aid in pulling them up if the first sleds down don't make it
past the planetary forcefield.

The helmets they're wearing have computer animations guiding
the eyes of the officers and displaying the locations of each officer.
It's also displaying the forcefield surrounding the planet.

The first two Scorpion commandos penetrate the forcefield and are
zipping into the atmosphere. Garrett is waiting for the bunker forcefield
to go down. Cyrus is not yet through the planetary forcefield. The third
officer collides with the forcefield and is incinerated. The hearts of the
remaining officers are pounding. The fourth officer chokes due to fear.
He jerks his sled too much and is incinerated. The fifth officer makes it

through. The other officers who make it through are screaming to the officers above the forcefield to keep the sleds inline and straight. Cyrus and Amelia are the last ones and are headed for the forcefield. Loud breathing is heard! They both make it through! Cyrus asks Garrett.

"Garrett are you locked onto all of us?"
Yes, Sir, but I need to beam you now! You're moving out of range."

Cyrus speaks to Heinrich through the cortical node:
"Heinrich, drop the bunker shield now!"

Heinrich is standing near a young male officer at the control station inside the bunker.

He walks up behind him and grabs his head and breaks his neck by snapping his head around to the left. The officer falls over dead. Heinrich gets onto the console and drops the bunker forcefield.

Garrett sees that the bunker forcefield is down and beams all the Omicron officers into the bunker.

The first officer who is closest to the bunker is too far out of range of the Antares. The Antares cannot lock onto him through the planetary forcefield. The officer's alarm is going off. He parachutes out and lands on the ground. He doesn't make it inside the bunker.

Only four Scorpion officers make it inside the bunker including General Cyrus Urlex and Commander Amelia Varren.

Cyrus and his team materialize inside the bunker and immediately start killing people using knives, guns, and their bare hands.

Cyrus is vicious and remarkable in battle. He moves like a machine. They're moving quickly through the bunker killing people. Several bodies lie dead on the floor.

None of the dead are cabinet members.
The cabinet members are hiding in the rear of the bunker.

The Apollyon undocks. The Betelgeuse beams the Apollyon ship with the extraction team inside into low orbit around Planet Nix. It rematerializes in space like a phantom out of thin air.

Chief Engineer Royce Allen quickly confirms that the Betelgeuse and the Apollyon are properly aligned to relay and amplify the Jinas transporter system. He makes a small adjustment to boost the power now that ships are in their final positions.

The team is standing inside the Apollyon ready to beam down into the bunker. Maia Elsu locks onto the team members. They all successfully materialize inside the bunker. They jump right into the fight. Cyrus quickly kills Captain Gerard Maddox with his bare hands.

Ben attacks Cyrus! They're going back and forth throwing each other around the room. Ben gets two strong shots in. Cyrus suddenly performs some extraordinary martial arts moves with his elbows and knees catching Ben off-guard. Ben collapses on the floor.

Chief Allen reports up to Raiden.

"Lord Raiden, Gerard is dead! Ben is down! General Urlex is here! He's killing everyone!" Raiden can hear the madness. Four people in the bunker turned out to be Omicron double agents helping Cyrus including Heinrich. Andrea and Mildred are fighting their way to Quinten and the other cabinet members in the rear.

Andrea and Amelia are locked in a fierce fight with each other. Both of their martial arts techniques are incredible. Amelia has a lightning-fast round kick. Raiden is stunned while listening to it all. Finally, he's heard enough! "Kira, you're with me! Maia, beam me and Kira down at once!" says Raiden. "Aye, Sir," says Maia.

"Qurel, you now have command of the ship," says Raiden.

Raiden and Kira stand-up and dematerialize from the bridge and rematerialize inside the bunker. They immediately join the fight.

Raiden runs up to Ben who is still lying on the floor but coming around. Kira, with a blade in each hand, is skillfully killing the Omicron double agents. She is a master with blades. Raiden stands up and runs after Cyrus. Amelia jumps in between. Amelia is a deadly killer. Raiden takes apart Amelia in five brilliant moves. She drops dead on the floor. Cyrus screams and goes berserk and runs after Raiden. Amelia was Cyrus's secret concubine.

Raiden and Cyrus are in a vicious brawl. Ben and Mildred kill the two remaining Omicron Scorpion officers. Royce and Andrea get to the cabinet members and are placing honing devices on them. Heinrich comes up behind Royce and stabs him in the back. Royce turns around and in three blazing-fast moves kills Heinrich with great force. Quinten is in shock that Heinrich was an Omicron traitor.

Raiden and Cyrus and are still going at it. It's an amazing fight.
Cyrus lands two good shots on Raiden. Raiden is injured and leaning
against the wall. Cyrus turns and runs for the cabinet members. He
pushes Royce aside and tackles Quinten. Raiden gets up and runs to
Cyrus and Quinten. Royce uses his android power and throws Cyrus
across the room. Cyrus slams against the wall. Andrea runs up to
Quinten, grabs onto him, and disappears with him. Mildred gets to
Mirren and they beam back. Kira beams back with two other cabinet
members. All the cabinet ministers are now safely on the Betelgeuse.

The only people left are Raiden, Royce, and Cyrus. Cyrus is
fighting both at the same time. Cyrus is a metahuman. He is so good
that he's simultaneously giving them both a good fight.

Raiden sees that everyone is safely beamed up. He makes a
brilliant set of moves on Cyrus knocking him to the ground allowing
himself and Royce a chance to beam back to the Betelgeuse.

Cyrus is left alone in the bunker with multiple dead Omicron
officers and no cabinet members. He screams while on his knees!
"NOOOO!!!"

The Antares is orbiting Nix while the Apollyon is in a
geosynchronous orbit.

The Apollyon comes into view of the Antares.
Garrett sees the Apollyon in space.

The Antares computer is showing that the Apollyon is one of the
escaped Scorpion Mabbas vessels. Garrett immediately fires upon and
destroys the Apollyon. No one was on board.

Raiden and his team and all the cabinet members are now safely
onboard the Betelgeuse. Unfortunately, Captain Gerard Maddox was
killed in action. Cyrus rushes over to a console in the bunker. He looks
on the computer and sees the quantum trans-link frequency for the
Betelgeuse which Mirren and Raiden had spoken on earlier.

The Betelgeuse is getting ready to go to warp. Raiden is just sitting
in his chair in between Qurel and Kira. Cyrus is hailing the Betelgeuse.
Lieutenant Maia Elsu speaks

"Lord Raiden, we're receiving a hail from the bunker on Nix."
"On screen, Maia," says Raiden.

❖ PLANET NIX ❖

General Cyrus Urlex appears large on the viewscreen of the Betelgeuse. He sees Raiden and the crew including Kira, Ben, and Royce who he was just fighting in the bunker. He also sees Quinten, Mirren, Andrea, Mildred, and two other Scorpion cabinet members. He is visibly furious! He speaks:

"Lord Raiden Bellatrix.
The Orion Empire committed a terrible crime against Scorpius today!
You did this! Not me!
Know this!
Scorpius and Orion are now officially at war!
We are coming for you!
It won't be just Scorpion ships upon your shores!
Oh, no! It will be much, much, worse!
The Omicron are everywhere!
We are already beyond your stargates!
We are in and among your most sacred places!
I will strike at the heart of the Empire!
I will not just kill you! First, I will make you suffer!
I will take everything you treasure most!
Until we meet again!"

End Transmission

Lord Raiden speaks to Maia while raising his hand to go to warp:

"Maia, Bellatrix Star System - Engage!"

To be Continued
Episode 2 - Coming Soon!

Made in the USA
Coppell, TX
19 July 2021

59196548R00094